I0667889

# Convergence of Evil Copy

## A 9/11 Story - First Edition, Limited Edition
### September 11th 2025
### Mark N. Klett

TIB

# *Foreword*

These forewords were graciously contributed by two retired U.S. Navy admirals who held critical posts during the events of 9/11.

---

I have known Mark my entire adult life. He is by nature a quiet guy, but one personality trait shines through constantly – he is a thinker. He thinks about things in a unique way to come up with novel solutions to complex problems. I see a lot of that trait in Convergence of Evil, weaving together history, fiction and the unknown to make the reader think about things they perhaps have not considered before, which makes it an enjoyable and entertaining read. Mark's professional life has prepared him well to write this book, providing solid first-hand experiences on which to draw. He draws the reader into a complicated world that no one has ever seen, but is real enough to believe. You will enjoy this book!
-**RADM Craig Quigley**, U.S. Navy (Ret.), Department of Defense Spokesperson at the Pentagon during 9/11

Having known Mark for many years, I know him to be an astute student of history, and geopolitical events. He is also a strategic thinker, but with the gift to translate that thinking into "here and now" realistic conclusions. In Convergence of Evil, he pulls together his perceptive knowledge of events that shaped history, and the strategic thinking that resulted, into a blend of "historical fiction" that is both thrilling and thought provoking. It will easily challenge your view of what is real, versus what is really possible. Given the suspected conspiracies that we read about daily, Mark weaves a story that will leave you questioning accepted history, know and conceivable government secrecy, and the profound conspiracy that is possible from it. Convergence of Evil is a masterful "page turner".

-**RADM Gary Jones**, U.S. Navy (Ret.), Commander of Naval Forces Korea during 9/11

This book is dedicated to the many people who have influenced my life and served with distinction in the military, each performing their roles with courage and integrity. To my roommates at the U.S. Naval Academy — thank you for the shared experiences, the long nights, and the lessons in discipline and leadership that helped shape the path ahead. To the junior officers who shared their insights and decision-making experiences with me...your loyalty, trust, and friendship are honors I carry with deep respect.

And to my friends and family, thank you for your steady support throughout this journey.

— Mark

# *Authors Note*

This novel is a work of fiction. While inspired by real-world events and shaped by the author's personal and professional experiences, it is a product of imagination, not a factual account. Events have been dramatized, timelines adjusted, and characters created or altered for narrative purposes. Some individuals in the story were inspired by real people, but names and details have been changed.

This book is not intended to disclose classified material or assert definitive truths. It reflects a creative interpretation of "what ifs" surrounding a critical moment in American history.

All historical images are used with permission from the National Archives and are presented with the utmost respect for the victims, survivors, and families affected by the tragedy of 9/11. The author extends deep reverence to those who served during this time and to those who continue to serve today.

# Dept of Defense Clearance Notice

# Convergence of Evil

## Mark N. Klett

# Contents

Prologue                                    1

1.  Intercepted Hints                       9

2.  Prelude to Chaos                        15

3.  The Attack                              24

4.  Shockwaves                              38

5.  The Liaison                             43

6.  Breadcrumbs                             47

7.  Black Projects                          54

8.  Men In Black                            68

9.  Echoes                                  73

10. The Unknown                             81

11. Threads Unraveling                      91

12. Decoding the Convergence               100

13. The Informant                          109

14. Government Secrets                      118

15. Alien Tech                             125

16. The Cover-Up                           134

17. First Contact                          153

18. Worlds Beyond                          160

19. Crossroads                             168

20. Technological Edge                     173

21. Web of Deceit                          177

22. Unlikely Allies                        182

23. The Battle Within                      187

24. Last Stand                             192

# *Prologue*

## June 2001- Afghan Mountains

The harsh Afghan sun glared relentlessly, the dry mountain air parching Farid's cracked lips. He squinted against the glare, surveying the rugged terrain through the scope of his rifle. The landscape of terracotta peaks and lush green valleys could conceal many threats, their movements so far evading unseen eyes. Foreign intelligence agencies scrambled to track their every step. Heat soaked through the layers of tactical gear, dampening his back as he dialed the satellite phone. Its weak encryption offered little protection from prying ears. Calloused fingers worked the keypad with practiced ease.

Nearby, his team guarded the herd of Arabi sheep, their hands gripped staffs that doubled as rifles. These men outranked simple shepherds, they emerged as tough fighters. Veterans of the Soviet war's brutal grind, their eyes tracked every ridge and shadow for signs of trouble. Now, a new conflict simmered below the surface, one that could shift the region's fate in ways no one could predict. Farid's call launched the plan. The secure line's weak encryption exposed their plot to foreign intelligence agencies with sharp ears and deadlier tech.

This was his land, his home, a silent witness to the conversations that would alter the course of history. While waiting for the signal to join the meeting, the other men tended the flock nearby.

Farid's call connected, and the voice on the other end spoke with a calmness that belied the storm of chaos they were about to unleash. He waved over his companions, each one chosen for their unwavering commitment to the cause. Among them was Tariq, a former engineer who turned militant, whose expertise had been pivotal in past operations. Then there was Khalid, a quiet man with a fierce intellect, who had masterminded the logistics of their plans.

As the men gathered around, Farid relayed the details of their latest conversation with Osama Bin Laden. The leader's words rang clear and direct, "We will not use trucks like in 1993. This time, the planes themselves become our bombs." The plan's boldness, its brilliant simplicity, sparked wildness in their eyes, a silent roar beneath their stares. Tariq, one of the few Osama trusted to wield the whispered 'trinity technology,' clenched his rifle-staff, stance rigid with intent. They sized up the job ahead, all of them filled with purpose. This climbed past a standard hit, it stood as a masterpiece, a genius stroke ready to rip history apart.

The sun sank below the horizon, stretching a warm blanket across the terrain. The air cooled, village sounds drifted up to the mountainside where the men hunched in a tight circle. Farid passed a large thermos of water, each man took a sip to ease his thirst. They shifted their weight, hands brushed rifles, every twitch hinting at the wreck they would spark. Tariq's voice cut through, "Farid, you really think this will work?" His words rasped with a strange thrill, doubt in his tone.

Farid nodded, kept like stone, concealing the truth inside. "It works because it has to," his voice stayed solid, covering the pretend he had become. "We've nailed every step, flight training, visas, timing, all set. With Allah's will, failures off the table." The words scraped him like sand, each one confirmed the doubt eating away at him. Deep down, he saw this plan, this bold stand, marking a sign across the world to haunt generations. Still, he pulled up straight, fixed his eyes ahead for the cause, for a truth he buried. A quick shadow hit his stare, something only he spotted. He squared himself, stuck to his role, driven by a purpose he alone held tight.

A murmur of agreement arose from the men, their eyes showing their dedication and consent. They sized up the risks, yet clung to the mission, their belief strong, cutting past hesitation. Talk shifted to logistics, each man took on in his role, spelling out his moves with precision. They kept their voices quiet, every word guarded, loyalty their shield.

July 2001- Maryland

Miles off, Maryland's intel bunker buzzed behind the unmarked 'green door,' a slab of steel and secrecy, walling off their covert grind. Inside the windowless hole, monitors flipped on, throwing a cold light over analysts as they dug in at their desks, out on the hunt.

The place was hopping. Encrypted data pouring in from everywhere. Phone intercepts in hundreds of languages fought the clack of keyboards chasing satellite feeds. Code scraps and busted signals warned of trouble closing in fast, details slipping every short reach.

Each analyst had a single chunk of the puzzle, eyeballing it hard to pull any bit of sense or link. Still, no one held the whole picture, that job fell to the hands steering this brutal intel chase. Leaders tossed most junior workers straight into the fire—they learned as they went. Fresh data constant, the crew kept pushing, aiming to stop whatever mess brewed out there.

Behind an angled semi-private wall, Amy Rockwell, a seasoned NSA analyst, stared at the data. She had been picking up a series of anomalies in the communications traffic, unusual spikes in talk among known terrorist cells. The messages were vague, peppered regarding a "new city" and an event of great importance. But without collaboration from other intelligence agencies, her findings remained just another set of scattered notes in an endless stream of info.

Amy rocked back in her chair, arms stretched high. She'd logged a lot of hours at her station, eyes pinned on everything new and old, digging through data. The patterns stood out, trouble she couldn't dismiss, yet without other agencies communicating, her catches would go nowhere. A pause, something off she couldn't pin down. She pictured their scattered efforts screwing them. They sat in silos, missing the full picture.

July 2001- Afghanistan

In the mountains, the men hashed out the plan's final pieces. Farid and his crew recalled their meeting with Osama Bin Laden, every word stuck clear. A Saudi, Bin Laden holed up in these Afghan hills, the rough ground masking his tracks. His family name packed wealth and pull, earning nods around here, his ventures propped up the locals. He spoke of righteousness, hammering their cause as just, their win a sure thing.

They'd huddled close, sheep stink and dust filled the air, Bin Laden mapped out their jobs. He'd drill down on precision, every move planned, no detail left loose. 'Timing's everything,' he'd repeat, 'execution takes it or breaks it.' The men bow their heads, full of grit and nerves. They saw their role as more than a hit, a loud jab at the West, their beliefs unbudgeable. The load of it a rough haul they lugged with pride and dread.

As they spoke, the sounds of the village faded into the background, replaced by sureness in their shared determination. The men prayed together, their voices rising in unison, a powerful display of their commitment. They believed a higher power supported their actions.

July 2001- Florida

In Florida, training took a darker turn. At a small-town flight school, middle eastern men drilled on commercial jet controls. They were cut with focus as they worked on the simulators' dashboards of switches. Their real aim stayed hidden from most. Paul Keogh, a CIA operative, chased a lead, a tip hitting his desk, a sour ex-instructor's note about the men's odd moves, their dodge of small talk, their grind on takeoffs and landings long after they'd nailed the basics. Keogh first shrugged it off, pegged it as cultural quirks, but the report stuck, itching under his skin. He scoped the school himself, slipping in, posing as a wannabe student. He clocked their drills, moves cool and sure, eyes fixed on the training, purpose rolling off them. A cold crept up, his intuition screaming, they aimed at something ugly.

Keogh always caught the odd stitch. His instincts pinged trouble fast, these guys drilled big jets over basic wings, the Posse Comitatus Act boxed him out from stepping in. He jotted his take, their focus and number of extra hours, not flight school fluff. That cold itch grew, but with agencies not talking, his notes just sat, trapped in his files.

Keogh often found himself at odds with the bureaucratic nature of intelligence work. He had spent years in the field where quick decisions and decisive actions were the norm. Now, regulations and protocols bound him, leaving him feeling powerless. He watched the flight school students with a growing sense of urgency, but without the cooperation of government, he believed his warnings would go unheeded.

July 2001- Maryland

In Maryland, Amy plugged away, irritated over the agencies' stonewalling. The CIA and FBI, set in their old grudge match, choked off info swaps. Each outfit clung to its stash, guarding sources, hiding tricks. Hidden within the mess were key scraps, while the greater stakes slipped past undetected.

Amy worked on the intel bits she had. The 'new city' mentions bugged her, maybe tied to old jobs or hits. Without a plan, without cross agency talk, her picks went nowhere, sunk in the pile. Nobody cared.

July 2001- Afghanistan

The planners kept the terrorist cells apart, each blind to the others' moves. This setup assured operational security. From Afghanistan's hills to America's packed streets, sleeper cells sat quiet, primed for the go signal. Osama Bin Laden held the reins, a dark hand steering them, keeping every crew rehearsed, ready. He knew their shot hinged on hitting together, nailing the enemy's core with synced strikes.

Osama's hold on the men stood remarkable. He'd cast their mission as a holy call, a jihad dragging them to honor and death. Their voices rose together in prayer, a powerful, unified sound. Convinced their actions were divinely guided, they felt justified.

The Soviet Afghan War, years back in the '80s, kicked off this mess when Moscow rolled tanks into Kabul. The U.S. jumped in, backed Afghan fighters, Bin Laden among them, tossing guns, cash, training to shove the Soviets out. That move cut both ways, forged ties that flipped hostile, a backfire stinging the States years later.

The Afghan landscape, once a battleground for Cold War proxies, had become a breeding ground for a new warfare.

Up in the mountains, the men discussed the meticulous plans. Planes as bombs smashed through doubt, a simple play that would break the game. The setup knotted up ugly, a slog of timing, visas, training, they had ironed out every kink. They knocked flasks together, grinning with confidence. The work was done. The strike was set. No turning back.

August 2001- Maryland

In Maryland's intel hub, Amy's irritation had been building. She hunched over reports, half put together with notes Paul Keogh had sent up, the new point man roping agencies into line. A decorated vet who never missed a trick. His latest could be something... a Florida flight school, middle eastern men drilling moves too out of line for any pilot run. His write up screamed trouble loud enough to wake the dead. She sifted the files, every piece an orphan, none snapping tight.

Amy worked her magic. Keogh's report and the men's behavior felt deeply unsettling. Every intel scrap fell flat, left her on empty, she'd flagged it, sent it up, got no pull, the quiet sank her leads.

She stalked the stacks for any clue she missed. Balled up looseleaf covered the floor, coffee cups stacked everywhere waiting to become trash, the bulbs overhead stayed always on, pinning her in place. She caught noise of "new city," a "trinity" thread from Kabul, plane counts off the books, scraps that didn't fit, piling up blind.

Amy continued, Keogh's report earned attention, those flight school drills spelling a blow nobody else caught. She'd bark it up the chain, hit deaf ears at every desk, the agencies too split to see it roll in. She faced the clock, time running thin, her warning lost.

# One

## *Intercepted Hints*

Paul Keogh lived inside routine, each day grinding forward in the same pattern he no longer questioned. He woke every morning at 5:30 a.m., his internal clock clicking on without fail. Soft early light filled his modest apartment, casting through the 600 square foot space, stretching over the worn carpet and a handful of unpacked boxes he hadn't bothered with since moving in. Paul sat on the sofa bed, running a hand through his graying hair, as thoughts of the day became a monkey on his back. Today was tougher than most, a challenge he could already feel was too much.

Paul put on his favorite white shirt and dark trousers. He ran through the divorce papers on the kitchen counter, black ink standing out against the pristine white paper. He had been avoiding this moment for weeks, but there was no more time left to delay. His soon-to-be ex-wife, Deborah, deserved closure, and he wanted to give it. He picked up the papers, his fingers brushing over her signature at the bottom of the page. Regret crept in, but he shoved it back. Today was his new life.

At the attorney's office, Paul sat across from his lawyer, Mark, who saw his share of "new starts" over the years. "You sure about this, Paul?" Mark asked, gentle yet probing, looking for any sign of hesitation.

Paul gave the OK, keeping his demeanor business, not showing the failure he felt inside, "It's for the best, Deborah deserves a better life than I can offer her, my new work takes everything I've got, she needs someone who can be there. I can't be that man anymore."

Mark let out a sigh, gathering the papers with breakfast still hanging on his hands, sealing them into a folder as if closing a chapter. "Well, if you're certain, I'll file these today, take care of yourself, Paul."

Paul manages to smile. "Thanks, Mark." He stood up, waved, avoided shaking the attorney's hand before leaving the office. As he walked out into the streets of Washington, D.C., his phone rang in his pocket. He pulled it out, seeing Brian Strohm's name flash on the screen.

"Brian, what is the current situation?" Paul says calm, despite his internal turmoil.

"Paul, we need you at the Pentagon, now, something's come up, and it's serious." The tension in Brian's voice, a rare thing, made Paul uneasy.

"I'll be there in twenty minutes," Paul replied, his mind all over the place. As Paul stepped into the cab, his thoughts shifted from Deborah's signature to the looming threats Brian had hinted at days before.


August 2001- Washington D.C.

Paul moved through the Pentagon's winding corridors, flashing his badge through each checkpoint. He stepped into a conference room where Brian waited and a current of urgency crackled through the room. Brian greeted him with a solid handshake, "Glad you could make it, we've got a situation, intelligence reports are piling up with chatter from terrorist networks, they're pointing to something big, something close."

Paul settled into a chair. "What kind of info are we hearing, anything distinct?"

Brian shook his head. "Not much yet, it's coded tight, we're picking up 'city of something,' 'event of great importance,' 'planes' in the mix, we need you to help sort through it."

In the Pentagon conference room, Paul and Brian sat opposite each other, their conversation laced with tension, the stale coffee and underlying unease, undeniable. He stared at the table strewn with redacted intelligence reports, their pages a jumble of code, his mind already systematically analyzing the possibilities. Every cryptic phrase a job, chipping away at his calm, building frustration he couldn't ignore.

Paul narrowed in. "Planes? Which aircraft are you referring to? Are we talking about airliners? Or something else?" He couldn't help thinking about his recent visit to the flight school in Florida but let the focus go to the new information he had in front of him.

Brian, empty of answers. "That's what we're chasing, we're pulling every resource we've got, we need to move fast."

Paul read through the latest intelligence updates, hovering over a line of coded text. More mismatched clues, each word exposing a deeper, more calculated danger. Closing in, pressure building with every line. If they didn't stop whatever it was now, the consequences may be irreversible.

Amid the doom and gloom, Paul thought about Deborah. He wondered if she was safe, if she had moved on with her life. The thought of her being caught in the crossfire of whatever was coming worried him. He had to stop this, not just for his job, but for her.

Hour by hour, the team uncovered more of the plot. Time slipped away, but Paul refused to relent. He would stop this attack, protect the people he cared about, and fulfill his duty as a CIA operative-no matter the cost.

Paul's phone goes off again during all the grind, a message from Amy Rockwell popping up, a lead analyst he'd teamed with before—short, urgent: "Paul, I think I've found something, we need to talk." He knew it was serious, she didn't call like that unless it was important.

Paul mapped out a trip to Maryland, every second counted, the drive time from the Pentagon to the NSA offices stretched longer than he liked. He couldn't waste a moment, so as soon as he could break free, he hit the road, thinking about what Amy might have uncovered, questions stacking up.

August 2001- Maryland

Paul and Amy sat in her cramped office, surrounded by cabinets and grouped intelligence reports. Amy pulled up the latest data. "I've been analyzing the intel we've picked up, and I think I've found a pattern," she said, keeping her focus on the screen.

Paul his interest piqued. "What kind of pattern?"

A series of coded messages appeared on the screen, Amy pointed to them. "These mentions of a "new city," an "event of great importance," this "trinity" bit about stealth planes, I think they're planning something big, this one feels different. I keep finding odd stuff, new phrases we haven't heard before, it's not sitting right, it's linking up in some way I can't place."

Paul studied the data. "Do we have any idea where or when?"

Amy looked at him. "Not yet, but we're getting there. The pieces are starting to fit together. We just need more time."

Paul took charge. "Then let's get to work. We don't have a moment to lose."

As they worked on the intelligence, Paul felt something building up, all this to an unknown deadline. Amy's skills and his experience are their only shot.

Work had always shaped Paul Keogh's life, but today, more than ever, that duty was hard against him, hurried and unyielding. A deadly plot unraveled in front of him, threads slipping loose, his job to tie them off. As he and Amy pushed late into the night, his mind lingered on the people he fought for, a danger he couldn't yet name.

The pieces started bridging, each hint bringing Paul and Amy closer to a trouble they couldn't grab hold of. Time ran short, their skills and grit the only wall against a strike they had to head off, no matter how fast it came.

As morning approached, Paul and Amy kept going with steady fire, so close to sorting out this mass threat. They'd jump fast when it clicked, hold back whoever was out there plotting doom, stand firm for the country they'd promised to keep safe.

A nameless danger pressed on Paul, growing louder, more urgent, despite his inability to identify it. He stood dead in for whatever waited, refusing to ease up until he'd stopped the evil rushing in.

# Two

## *Prelude to Chaos*

September 2001- Washington D.C.

Paul Keogh, his face starkly lit by the fluorescent lights of the CIA's main office, leaned over his desk, which was submerged under stacks of paperwork. His eyes, red and weary from hours of digging, focused on pages filled with analysts' annotations, noting the growing chatter within terrorist networks and the persistent recurrence of the term "trinity."

Paul gave his all-working to crack the real meaning of these coded messages. He saw time slipping away, the pieces holding back, unwilling to budge. He had a car waiting to pick him up and got ready to go, throwing reports into a bag. As a seasoned liaison linking the CIA and other departments, Paul had built a reputation for smart insights, negotiation, pulling agencies into line, skills he'd need now more than ever.

Across the city, Secretary of Defense Brian Strohm power-walked through the corridors, his presence alone underscoring the gravity of the situation. His face bore marks of long military experience, a testament to the countless crises he'd managed, geopolitical storms he'd weathered. Even now, with the weight of the potential catastrophe bearing down on him, Brian's commitment to physical and mental readiness never wavered. He'd taken the stairs instead of the elevator, already thinking about what he'd share at the meeting. Every step, every moment, offered a chance to stay ready, to brace for whatever challenges lay ahead. Even if he was alone in them.

The Pentagon's War Room, officially the National Military Command Center, had its share of crises through the years. From the Cuban Missile Crisis to Operation Desert Storm, this nerve center had anchored some of America's toughest military calls. Today, however, the War Room, usually marked by order and control, is full of rushed action unlike anything seen in recent history.

High-ranking officials from every military branch gathered around the conference table. General Joe Laffey, chairperson of the Joint Chiefs of Staff, stood at the head, his hard stare showing the seriousness of the moment. Beside him, the chiefs of each service-Army, Navy, Air Force, Marines, lined up tight. Their being there carried the full heft of the trouble brewing.

The civilian leadership stood just as strong. The CIA Director spoke privately with the FBI Deputy Director, their usual agency squabbles dropped fast as trouble threatened them. Senior officials from the National Security Agency crowded over laptops, pumping real-time data straight to the gathered brass.

The conspicuous absence of the nation's two highest-ranking officials created a void. The President stayed in Florida, gearing up for public stops, a school visit set to read to kids the next day in Sarasota. The Vice President, typically present at these meetings, tackled urgent talks with energy sector heads, digging into critical infrastructure worries. Their absence, even for important reasons, piled extra strain onto an atmosphere already pricked with unease.

This meeting was super intense, way different than usual. Voices battled, sparking worried whispers, but all resolved. Analysts zipped in and out, dropping updates, picking up fresh orders. They all knew this was a big deal, you only see this kind of panic when trouble's brewing.

Secretary of Defense Brian Strohm's arrival silenced the room. All eyes moved in his direction, searching for a lead against a threat nobody'd seen coming. History's load brought an echo of big calls made right there that had changed nations' paths. Now, once more, countless lives rested on this room, hinging on what these men and women chose in the hours ahead.

Paul was hesitant as he stepped into the War Room. Everyone wanted answers and that need pushed him against a wall. Theories abound, each one screaming important. Beneath this solid front, though, doubt chewed at Paul constantly. The gathering of amazing minds only amplified the deep dread in Paul. This wasn't your typical mess, it possessed a dark, insidious undercurrent. The inescapable feeling that they were facing something deceptively wicked, something that could easily outwit them all, settled upon him. Nausea rolled through him, his body revolting against the constant unease. His fear was for the country and its innocent people, not himself. He inhaled.

Brian called the room to order, slicing through the chaos. "Ladies, gentlemen, we're facing a threat unlike anything we've met before, the intelligence points to multiple, coordinated strikes tearing at U.S. soil. We need answers, we need them fast."

Paul feels under scrutiny. Adrenaline fueled his anxiety, but he still found himself saying, "We're seeing a pattern."

He waved at the screens showing the intercepted communications. "The encrypted communications are intensifying and highly sophisticated, exceeding anything previously analyzed. The recurring theme of a "trinity," alongside inconsistent terminology, is unlike anything in our terrorist databases."

Questions and guesses flew around the room like a storm. Brian silenced the noise with a gesture of his hand. "We must combine all our resources, personnel, and expertise; the more people working on this, the better chance we have of deciphering their plans before time runs out." His eyes scanned the room, piercing each person with his stare. "We're launching a unified task force right away, abandoning agency barriers to operate as one team and eliminate this threat."

The day wore on, and the intelligence analysts worked intensely, decoding messages and sending a constant stream of reports to the War Room. Rumors circulated about several high-profile targets nationwide, all connected to a mysterious "new city." The pattern of attacks on core American symbols remained maddeningly unclear due to a lack of information. Tick-tock, tick-tock...the War Room knew a battle was coming.

While Washington analysts worked diligently, terrorist cells were secretly mobilizing worldwide. They each worked alone, oblivious to the others, and sent reports to Osama Bin Laden. He controlled them with a cold, firm hand, manipulating them from the darkness.

A rare piece of signals intelligence revealed a previously unheard message from Bin Laden. The NSA's sharpest systems nabbed a slice of it, the encryption tougher than anything they'd run up against before.

"The stars line up,' Bin Laden's voice rasped. 'When the eagle's wings get clipped, the world will tremble. Your shadows in place yet? Everything set for the eagle's drop."

The words held clues about attacks to come, but we didn't know who or what would be targeted. "Could it be a bomb?", Amy wondered. Brian went along with it once he got her report.

Paul, in his Pentagon office, recalled the Soviet Afghan War, recognizing it as the root of the current crisis. The U.S. backed Afghan fighters, a young Bin Laden among them, in their stand against Soviet troops. That help, handed out for strategy's sake, ended up arming Bin Laden, stoking his hate for the West.

Paul shared his insights with Brian. "Bin Laden's personal vendetta against the West is driving this," Paul mused. "He sees us as a threat to their way of life, their beliefs, their power. That's what's motivating them."

Brian's look grew somber. "We underestimated the intensity of his hatred and his manipulative nature, it's not merely ideological, it's deeply personal."

As night fell, Paul landed back at CIA headquarters, the War Room's strain trailing him across town. He needed his best analysts to stitch the parts, to plug the holes that might stop whatever was attempting to break in.

"Paul, sir, look at this," David, one of the lead analysts, called out. He pointed to a line of code on his screen. "This phrase here, 'new city' keeps coming up. It's almost like they're using it as a codename for something."

Paul leaned closer, a frown creasing his forehead. "New city, new city... Yes, that sounds familiar."

David shrugged. "We've run it through all our usual decryptions, but nothing fits. It's like they're speaking in riddles."

Paul's eyes lit up. "Nostradamus," he said under his breath.

"What?" David looked puzzled.

"Nostradamus. The 16th-century seer who wrote cryptic prophecies. What if the terrorists are using similar cryptic language to throw us off?" Paul not amused.

AS David set to work cross-referencing Nostradamus' works with the intercepted code phrases, Paul's thoughts drifted to his days studying ancient texts and ciphers. Little did he know then how crucial that knowledge would become now.

September 2001- Afghanistan

Halfway across the globe, in a dim compound tucked into Afghanistan's ancient mountains, Osama Bin Laden met with his lieutenants. The air sagged thick with incense, soft prayer murmurs blending in. Bin Laden's eyes, sharp, pierced the room.

"We sit on the cusp of what nobody expects," he started. "The infidels grew soft, they think they stand untouchable. We'll prove their weak spots."

Khalid, one of his lieutenants, yelled out to the crowd. "The cells stand ready, each team knows its mission, its target, we've burned this into them, they're set to lay down their lives for the cause."

Bin Laden's gaze swept the room once more. Music jammed. He went on..."Remember, this is not just an attack. It is a message. We are striking at the heart of their arrogance, their hubris. Allah is with us, and we cannot fail."

September 2001- Washington D.C.

A tired but determined Paul and Brian met at the Pentagon that morning, as the sun came up over Washington. The joint task force plugged away all night, their stubborn push finally paying off.

"We've nabbed something," Paul points to an image. "David matched Nostradamus to the chatter and one passage jumps out," 'In the new city, a big disaster hits, when the two brothers drop, the world slides into mercy.'

Brian threw his hand up. "New York? The "two brothers, could those point to big buildings there?"

Paul says. "It fits. They're using Nostradamus as a framework for their code. The 'new city' could peg New York. And the 'two brothers'... it might be symbolic, but we can't be certain yet."

"If that holds, we need to move quick," Brian mutters, already grabbing his secure phone. "We can't risk losing any leads, I'm pulling in every asset we've got." Brian never dialed the phone.

Paul knew they stood so close to uncovering the full reach of the terrorists' plans. When they did, they'd be ready to act, to stop the attack in its tracks, to guard the nation they'd sworn to defend.

They raced against time, pushing them to shove past exhaustion, frustration and fear.

With the rising sun, coffee began to brew. Paul and Brian exchanged a meaningful look. The toll of sleepless nights and the burden of their responsibilities were evident in their eyes, which met Paul's with an expression of trust. The air between them hung with iron will.

Seated within the austere confines of the War Room, they recognized the world's complete unawareness of their situation. Throughout the country, individuals engaged in their morning routines—coffee consumption and newspaper review—oblivious to the escalating peril. This gap further burdened their mission. Clueless civilians depended on people like Paul and Brian to shield them from a threat they couldn't identify. That truth hit them hard, so they kept going.

Every new fact hit them hard but also fired them up. With a full awareness of the risks involved and the time sensitivity of the situation, they silently recommitted to using every ounce of strength to proceed. Failure was not an option.

The breakthrough energized the task force. Analysts searched intel for hidden codes. FBI agents quickly assessed threats to aid local police. Their goal remained steadfast: to issue a strong warning quickly once the impending threat was identified, all while avoiding mass panic.

Paul, powered by caffeine and nerves, coordinated everything. High stakes fueled their race against whatever they were fighting. Seeing those dedicated people working so hard filled him with pride.

They made some progress, but he still wondered if it was enough.

# Three

## *The Attack*

The morning broke with a true blue, clear sky stretching over New York City. Streets kept on, full of the steady beat of commuters, vendors, and tourists. Among them strode Larry Evans, a seasoned firefighter with Engine 10, Ladder 10, posted just a heartbeat from the World Trade Center.

You couldn't tell from Larry's calm exterior how much he'd been through. He was a Vietnam vet, tough as nails, and he'd seen it all. Though wounded by war, he emerged stronger, fiercely protective and dedicated to service. Back from Vietnam, Larry put those instincts into firefighting, finding his calling in charging toward danger as others ran. His military roots gave him a backbone of discipline and a knack for teamwork, marking him as a leader at the firehouse.

The sun crept up, painting the city in a warm amber. It was a stunning September morning, a soft breeze whispering of fall's approach. Larry nursed his coffee, trading stories with his crew, who couldn't help but note the day's beauty.

"Wish summer'd stick around, especially with mornings like this," one of them tossed out, eyeing the endless blue overhead. A relaxed atmosphere surrounded them, as New Yorkers, embodying their city's resilient spirit, basked in the pleasant weather and the potential of a bright day.

September 11th 8:46 a.m. - New York City

As Larry breathed the crisp autumn air outside the firehouse, a monstrous blast and thunderous roar shattered the peaceful morning, making the ground shake violently beneath his boots. He experienced a profound, instinctive fear; its impact was immediate and physically jarring, evidenced by his accelerated pulse. Adrenaline. He caught sight of the North Tower through the open station doors; once a monument of power and pride, it was now breached, a gaping wound from which black smoke ascended like a malevolent serpent. A look of stunned disbelief contorted his features, his mouth hanging open in a silent gasp, his breath seemingly stolen by the sight before him. A scream replaced the day's beauty, freezing the world in terror.

The firehouse was in utter chaos. Larry's coffee cup slipped from his hand and smashed on the floor, its contents spilling like a faded hope. Alarms blared, men shouted over each other, and sirens closed in fast, wiping out the station's usual rhythm. He suddenly got it. Shaking, he grabbed his stuff, he had a bad feeling about what was outside.

Outside, everything went to hell. Folks were glued to the pavement, their faces showing pure shock. A noxious mixture of burnt fuel and scorched metal filled the air, a harsh indicator of the calamity. Larry's thoughts were unfocused, his sense of duty struggling against overwhelming fear. He met the eyes of his crew, their usual talk replaced by a silent, powerful vow. This was it, the terror they'd hoped would never come, the hardest test they'd ever meet.

As they suited up, the truth slammed into them with brutal force. They were heading into a war zone, a place of unimaginable ruin. A mournful cry rolled through the streets, the roar of engines cutting into the city's broken heart.

The trip to the World Trade Center seemed to drag on, despite being quick. What were once lively streets were now a scene of utter pandemonium, cars blocked the roads, pedestrians scrambled in all directions, and emergency vehicles desperately tried to get through. Larry saw the North Tower — all torn up, a hole in the sky. Flames shot up, a terrifying, sky-high inferno.

They were hit by intense heat as they neared, a huge wall of fire, consuming the air. That horrible smell of burning jet fuel made Larry's lungs burn, he had to move fast, seeing people falling from the building. His mind raced to his wife, his folks, and loved ones, none of them knew what a mess he was in. He pushed the thought aside and focused on the mission. They had lives to save from the jaws of hell.

The fire trucks screeched to a stop, and Larry and his team leaped out, their boots thumping on the pavement. They stood at the brink of the abyss, a place no sane person would willingly enter. One last look at his comrades, Larry braced himself and walked toward the North Tower.

Getting closer to the North Tower, everything felt unreal, like a film. Everyone was running and looked terrified. Larry was completely shocked. The plane's impact left its brutal mark on the once proud tower, shredding the steel and glass, and spewing flames and thick black smoke from the fresh gash.

As Larry entered the burning tower, memories of Vietnam surged through his mind. The smell of smoke, the cries of the injured, the horror all echoed with unwelcome familiarity. Vivid flashes of jungle hell gripped him, the screams of the wounded and the stench of burning flesh from decades past ripping in his senses. But this time, he faced a towering inferno in the heart of New York City, not a battlefield of trees and mud. Larry tapped into his military training, shoving fear into a tight box and zeroing in on the mission. He knew every second mattered, and lives hung on his ability to stay focused and guide his team. His Marine training kicked in, driving him to face danger head-on and save everyone he could.

The tower's interior resembled hell. You couldn't breathe, the smoke from the jet fuel was so strong. People were screaming as Larry and his team struggled upwards. New terrors appeared on each floor, where dust-covered workers clung to one another, frozen in disbelief and terror. Tears streamed down the dirty cheeks. Loads of people, some coughing up a storm, others totally freaked out, crammed the hallways. Larry didn't stop, though. He had to rescue those people above.

September 11th 9:03 a.m. - New York City

A deafening sound hit. The North Tower shook, nearly throwing Larry off balance. He saw a fireball burst from the South Tower through a broken window.

"Oh God, not again," he kept to himself, wanting to scream out. People were calling out begging everywhere. That was deliberate. Larry looked at his team, and they were all on the same page. They faced an unseen enemy in a world of fire. Time was running out for their mission. "Go!" Above the panic, Larry's voice rang out. "Everybody get out, now!"

They fought their way past terrified office workers, moving forward against the tide. Larry directed people to the exits, yelling instructions as he tapped shoulders. He moved, gripped by cold certainty. They were still so far from the top.

September 11<sup>th</sup> 9:05 a.m. - Florida

Meanwhile, in Sarasota, Florida, the President of the United States sat in a brightly lit classroom at Emma E. Booker Elementary School, reading aloud to a group of young children. Their small faces turned up to him, caught in the story, while he kept his voice rhythmic despite the earlier news—a plane had struck the North Tower in New York City just minutes ago. Calmly focused on the page, he masked his inner tension, betraying nothing to those in the room. At 9:05 AM, the Chief of Staff whispered news of a second plane hitting the second tower. America was under attack. The President, though marked by an air of gravity, finished his story before rising to speak to the nation.

September 11$^{th}$ 9:20 a.m. - Washington D.C.

At the Pentagon, Secretary of Defense Brian Strohm sat in an emergency meeting, his mind sifting through the scraps of intelligence gathered over recent months. Murmurs of terrorist plans and unconfirmed warnings from the middle east stayed with him, details his team struggled to connect. The aides were on pins and needles around him, tons of questions hanging over their heads. With the news of a plane crash in New York City fresh, Brian sat immobile, his face a blank slate, a thought carefully concealed within his mind.

The FAA contacted the Department of Defense, sharing every detail they had on the attack and ordering all planes grounded. Brian was on top of it; halting air traffic was a smart move to gain control over what might come next. Questions piled up without answers, an unfamiliar future brewing. Would submarines creep toward the coast? Were hidden planes circling, ready to hit? Was the border secure?

9:37 AM. A roar erupted, and everything went crazy. The conference room shook violently. Coffee cups crashed to the floor. Instantly, Brian reacted, he dropped to the ground, pulling a dazed aide with him, the impact of hitting the hard floor jarring, under the heavy oak table. The explosion followed.

The western side of the Pentagon burst into a massive inferno. The blast rocked the building, shaking windows and hurling debris through offices. Fuel-soaked smoke poured through the vents, its bite signaling ruin.

From under the table, Brian heard the mayhem beyond the conference door. A rumble rolled through the walls, followed by a pop of glass shattering somewhere down the hall. Faint shouts bled through the wall as frantic footsteps pounded past. The air filled with a moan of a sinking metal ship, a sound that promised worse to come, all while the room itself held, spared from the fire coming through the western side.

"Dear God," Brian muttered, climbing out from under the table, annoyed. "We were too late." He straightened, brushing off debris, shook it out. Alarms screamed as he charged down corridors packed with confused personnel. His thoughts, organizing what he should share as the official story and what he should not. A step ahead of the panic around him. The murmurs, the hints, all falling on him to address, yet he buried that to the end of his thoughts, wearing the face everyone expected to see.

He burst into the Command Center, a mix of get done and circus. Data lines from across the globe spit out data, phones rang without end, and officers gave orders with a firm hand hoping everyone would get in line. Go, go, go.

"Status report, now!" Brian pissy, as if the room bent to his will.

As military officials hustled to gauge the damage and crafted a response, Brian watched with a cool detachment. The attack had exposed their sluggish pace, leads buried under layers of caution and red tape, and he would let it hang on their shoulders, not his. He stood above the fray unmoved by their fumbling.

Brian carried himself with arrogant sophistication, unfazed where others faltered. Submarines nearing the coast, unseen planes poised to strike, the border's strength, all questions he let swirl around him, his thoughts a step ahead, untouched by the doubt overcoming the room.

Brian understood their world had shifted permanently. A restlessness stuck with him, this was only the start. The task of unraveling to the public how they'd believe they missed it, and ensuring it never had to happen again was not an easy one. The convergence would have to be carefully controlled.

September 11$^{th}$ 9:57 a.m. - New York City

Short of breath, Larry climbed the North Tower. In the sweltering heat, sweat ran down their faces and immediately evaporated. Smoke shrank their world to a few inches, changing once familiar offices into a snarl of ruin.

Come this way! Larry's protest showed everyone that someone was in control. He climbed, the stairwell crammed with people, the desperation growing with each floor. He saw terrified people screaming in the hall-ways and offices. "I need help!", "I'm suffocating!", "How do I escape?" He pushed past people, pulling the wounded along, their weight slowing him, fighting to keep the evacuation moving. Panic and pleading etched ash- and blood-streaked faces. Every person saved was a small victory against the raging fire, yet countless others succumbed to the blaze and vanished.

Suddenly, the building started to move. You could hear the pain in the air.

September 11$^{th}$ 9:59 a.m. - New York City

Everything went quiet except for this crazy loud roar. The South Tower came crashing down, a huge, earth-shaking boom. Larry grabbed a pole as the North Tower swayed and lurched violently. He nearly went through the floor. He glimpsed the South Tower's destruction through a hole in the wall. Wild screams ripped through the smoky air. "It's gone!" "We're next!" Surrounding him, people stumbled, some retreating to offices, clinging to false senses of security. Larry knew time was almost up.

"Move! Move! MOVE!" Larry's yell ripped from his chest, fierce and desperate. Fear scraped his throat, but he swallowed it whole. People hung on his every word. His injured team pounded down the stairs, slumping, reaching for support as they dragged their wounded. As Larry descended, he felt a fleeting but undeniable sense of occupying the boundary between life and the afterlife, his spirit teetering on the precipice of mortality and eternity. It was survival or surrender. Forcing his way through the crowd, he neared the lobby, pulling others toward the exit. The building groaned, a sound like grinding stone and cracking timber, the deep vibrations shaking him as its end neared. Each step felt risky, the close front doors hidden within the inferno.

Terror reigned in the streets outside. A huge cloud of dust and debris from the fallen South Tower blocked out the sun. The unseen danger sent people scattering, their shoes pounding the pavement as they fled through crowds and smoke. Despite this, some people remained, shopkeepers staring blankly at their devastated shops, stunned and sorrowful, while office workers took shelter in nearby buildings, having been told to stay put for their safety. The haunting image of people jumping from high windows, dark shapes disappearing into the smoky air, was captured on countless phones and cameras, held by trembling hands. The North Tower swayed, burning and unsteady, a giant teetering on the brink.

September 11$^{th}$ 10:03 a.m. - Shanksville, Pennsylvania

United Airlines Flight 93 tore through the calm of rural Pennsylvania. The plane plunged from the sky, its final drop, a piercing scream of silver wind and engine. Ripping into a field near Shanksville, the plane dug out a massive crater with brutal force.

For a moment, fear blanketed the countryside. The quiet farmland, once alive with birdsong and the rattle of distant tractors, now rang with police sirens and stain of rage.

The loud boom sent residents rushing outside, bewildered and searching. Jet fuel's sharp smell stung them, replacing the clean country air. They checked on loved ones. Hands reached for phones, dialing quick, "You, okay? You hear that?" while others scanned their yards, counting heads—kids, dogs, livestock—needing to know all were safe.

Emergency personnel sped to the scene, tires spinning on the narrow roads. They came upon a mess of mangled metal and smoldering earth. The crater consumed the rolling fields, turning the earth inside out.

The crash caused immediate uncertainty and disbelief. Long-time residents unwillingly witnessed the tragedy. Everything shook, a growl hung in the air after the hit, and the sky got dark, foggy, and full of unanswered questions. They hid their faces behind scarves and coats so they wouldn't breathe in the fumes, warning neighbors close-by. The wreckage's heat was a stark contrast to the morning's breeze. Except for warnings, silence gave way to dropped jaws and worried faces. The evil in their world caused farmers to freeze, tools in hand, families to cluster on porches, and children to cling to their parents. One moment, it was a normal morning; the next, their quiet town was forever changed, with many lives—and heroes—lost.

September 11$^{th}$ 10:28 a.m. - New York City

Time ran out; the North Tower fell, shaking the city. Through mayhem and blind shoving, Larry and some of his team had reached the ground floor. The building creaked and swayed, and Larry felt like this was it. "Run!" he shouted, waving from the exit. With the manic energy of a madman, he shoved people out the doors and away from the collapsing giant, guiding them to safety.

The sound was like a wall of noise when the tower came down. A woman stumbled, and Larry reacted instantly; he threw himself on top of her to protect her as a thunderous sound filled the air. Wounded cried out as shards flew. Propped on one elbow, he waved his free hand, shouting, "Run! Keep going!" He willed himself, urging others to flee while he shielded her, death raining down.

As the dust cleared, New York's streets were hidden under a layer of debris. Ash and smoke made everything dirty and gray, and it was hard to breathe. The skyline, once crowned by the Twin Towers, stood empty where icons once had soared.

Larry emerged from the rubble, bruised, caked, his left arm throbbing from shrapnel by exploding steel. He stumbled, coughing, struggling to pull himself upright. His was in disbelief—he was alive, somehow whole despite the ache. Beneath him, the woman he'd shielded alive, her breaths shallow. With a grunt and shaky legs, he pulled her from the mess and dragged her to safety. He was overwhelmed by the devastation. He saw dazed survivors, the injured receiving aid, and the destroyed skyscrapers.

September 11$^{th}$ 11:30 a.m. - Washington D.C.

At the Pentagon, Brian evaluated the damage. The building's west side was blown open by a plane. Medics ran around, dragging wounded people to the ambulances waiting, shouting over the chaos as they lifted stretchers over the cracked road. The scene was horrifying, widespread fires and swirling black smoke, unmistakable evidence of a brutal and inescapable attack.

With clipped instructions and no margin for error, Brian directed his advisor on exactly what to tell the press before dispatching him to the parking lot and the waiting cameras. His voice remained even; his priority was to alleviate suffering without revealing too much.

A senior officer in command declared, "This is not a drill." A nearby colonel received Brian's signal to relay the order. Exercises along the east coast were in full swing, and some had mistaken the attacks for a test. Truth quickly dispelled the fog. With all flights grounded by authorities, American skies were left eerily empty—an unusual sight for a country accustomed to constant air traffic.

The terrorists had exploited a gap. They switched off the IFF transponders, dodging radar except for those close enough to see. That move had cleared their path, hitting hard with ruthless efficiency, and Brian took it in, thinking of who may have given that order, sizing up in his mind, who else was involved.

September 11$^{th}$ 11:59 a.m. - New York City

Lower Manhattan battled for air. People stumbled from the wreckage, many mumbling, half alive, clothes shredded and white by the fallout. For every soul staggering away, another rushed in, shoes crunching over glass, hands outstretched toward the smoking pile.

New Yorkers, in denial and wandering, desperately called anyone they knew who might be trapped. "Anyone in there?" "Where's my brother?" Desperate for a sign, they called out into the rubble, hoping for a sound, any sound, in return. With their bare hands, they ripped through the wreckage, searching for survivors. Water bottles and bandages were readily available to help stop bleeding and save lives.

Network overload; silent, desperate phones. The unanswered calls only added to the growing fear of missing family members.

Journalists set up single camera operations, dodging barricades, unsteady cameras recording the scene of mangled metal and destruction. Reporters, overcome with emotion, could barely speak, struggling to articulate the events as emergency vehicles blocked streets, isolating the scene.

The New York skyline slumped and broke. The city's pulse gone.

Standing amongst the ruins, Larry felt the nation's grief as his own, each breath a shared lament. The fallen men weighed heavily on his soul, their faces constantly flashing before his eyes, fueling a burning, stubborn anger at their senseless deaths. His Marine spirit fueled him. His perseverance would honor them.

Vietnam veteran Larry felt the day's toll. He'd led men through the horrors of war, the sights and sounds forever etched into his mind, but here, fueled by a primal instinct, he hauled people onto his back, driven by a desperate need to save them, ignoring the danger to himself. The cost hit him hard; lives beyond his help, screams he couldn't stop. The searing image of a man's face, consumed by fire, remained indelibly etched in Larry's memory, leaving an enduring mark on his psyche. He lived through it all, but it didn't feel real to him.

The world was devastated by 9/11. Even in tough times, Evans and others showed amazing strength, but the losses still hurt, and some things just can't be healed.

# Four

## *Shockwaves*

Lower Manhattan felt the sting of a dry, bitter wind. Amid the pleas of the injured and the sounds of desperate digging through rubble, firefighters and paramedics surged through the streets, their shouts echoing above the cries. A woman's sob was, "Where are they?" Shards of metal and debris spiked the ground, marking trails of red where the injured dragged or collapsed, a scene profound with loss.

Larry Evans trudged through the streets. His lungs burned with every gulp of air. Around him, survivors drifted, lost in a daze, their clothes torn, shoes melding into the sidewalk below.

"Over here!" Larry shouted, he spotted civilians crouching near a storefront, its front half caved in. He bolted toward them, when a shiver hit him. Something glinted in the rubble, a flash of metal that didn't belong. He froze for a heartbeat, torn between the huddled figures and the odd shine. A lady's cry yanked him forward; he rushed to her, shoving the mystery to the back of his mind for later.

The item again caught Larry's attention as he was turning away. He was consumed by curiosity. He stepped in, kneeling to sweep garbage aside. A molten gold triangle glowed from the wreckage, unlike anything he'd seen. Three faint, ethereal pulses of light pulsed in the corners, a strange and unsettling sight. It felt heavy, warm, and foreign in his hand. Instinctively, he pocketed the item, sensing its significance.

In the ruins, blocks from the scene, the normally outspoken mayor of New York City spoke sparingly, pushing through crowds toward a waiting podium. To a small group of reporters, a contrast to his usual polished press corps, he rasped, "We will rebuild," his words captured by New Yorkers amidst the chaos, their faces masked, their coughs punctuating the announcement. His unrehearsed message, heavy with the loss of his city, spilled out.

September 11$^{th}$ 3:45 p.m. - Washington D.C.

In the Pentagon War Room, Secretary Strohm monitored the crisis.

Demanding attention, he barked, "Give me the rundown!"

A junior officer stepped up, seeing the opportunity. "Sir, we're still piecing together the damage. Early counts point to heavy casualties. Unconfirmed intel's coming in too—possible other targets."

Brian's chest was puffed out from years of hard work, but he was annoyed by all the mess he had to clean up. "Other targets? Where?"

The officer answered. "Sir, it's murky. Word around say sleeper cells might be waking up nationwide. Nothing solid yet, but..."

Brian looked down at the stammering kid with contempt. "Keep me updated."

The officer hightailed it out of there, his heels clicking, while Brian just stood there, thinking.

Endless gym hours were evident as Brian, arms crossed, leaning against the command table, his muscles flexing beneath his suit. The room was filled with the sound of static voices as maps and live feeds, a flurry of red dots, scrolled across the screens. He was bothered by a nagging sense of something amiss. Surprisingly, the attacks effortlessly bypassed all security. Distracted and irritated, he gave a slight smirk, barely registering the triviality of the situation while larger, more pressing concerns filled his mind.

Brian scanned the reports, noticing every little thing. The hijackers simultaneously deactivated the planes' transponders, deliberately circumventing safety protocols. Before impact, electromagnetic bursts and unconfirmed static crackled near the targets. Satellite photos revealed fleeting, unexplained signals near the planes, defying identification. These quirks stacked up.

Now, with the attacks tearing every plan to shreds, those hints buzzed in his head. He knew the outline—Al-Qaeda was the face, but other things blurred. Something else? He'd only gotten drips, never the full pour. A word stuck out—trinity—murmured, vague and unclaimed.

His fingers curled around the secure phone, a quick flex before he dialed a number buried deep. "Amy? Brian. I need you on something, off record. You remember those trinity rumors, strange tech? Run it down. This hits too easy, and I'm not buying the surface story. Find out what it is, why I'm out of the loop."

He slammed the phone down, half-annoyed he had to dig through pawns for answers. If this trinity thing broke open, he'd lean on every trick he brushed against in those black project years. Whatever rolled in, he'd muscle it into place.

Deep below the White House, the Vice President, known for his greed and shady dealings, impatiently read the latest intelligence reports in a sealed bunker. The reports angered him; his grip tightened on each one.

With a sharp "Military flights only—ground all others!", he cut through the room's panic. "Set me up a line to the President. We're rolling out continuity plans now."

The day dragged on, and it became clearer how widespread the attacks were. The crashes were on TV, on repeat, burned into everyone's minds. The stock market bolted shut, its opening chime killed by the mess. Airports nationwide shut down, stranding travelers.

September 11<sup>th</sup> 7:11 p.m. - New York City

In New York's streets, a movement took root. Missing person photos were stuck on anything that stood still—walls, lampposts, the works. In every picture, a face stared back, its personality preserved, its name marked in pen, a desperate hope fighting against the city's descent into chaos.

Larry drifted toward these temporary shrines. He studied them, each one a life teetering between lost and found. A woman came up, her cheeks red, tears carving paths through them.

"Please," she asked, desperate. "My husband, 89th floor. Did you, anyone from up there see him?"

Larry felt paralyzed. He knew the odds, this stretched past impossible, but her look pinned him. "We're still searching," he said. "Hold on. We won't quit until we've turned over every stone."

Overwhelmed by his words, she sobbed, finding solace in them as she disappeared back into the crowd. Larry turned his head. Each person they rescued, living or dead, brought a measure of peace to those devastated by the tragedy.

Night fell, and the city went dark. Silent streets, only flashing lights and sirens broke the stillness. Ground Zero's void was brightly lit by floodlights.

Lost in the rubble, Larry stood alone, his fireman's hat nowhere to be found. Saved and lost faces clashed in his mind, an unbalanced ledger. Though not the jungles of Vietnam, this experience transformed him, stripping away his former self and forging a purpose—a guiding light for others in darkness.

# Five

## *The Liaison*

September 12$^{th}$ 8:00 a.m. -Washington D.C.

Paul Keogh sat at his desk, the sealed office air sharp with coffee and day-old cologne. Years in the CIA had made him tough, but this liaison role bridging agencies after yesterday's collapse piled a nation's grief on his back. He felt every life lost, every nightmare people were living and took it on to himself. Phones rang constantly, fax machines spit pages, and analysts barged in, dropping intel that burned his hands with every touch.

"What's real?" he asked, facing a room of tired officers', arms over messy stacks. "Six months back, every clue, every guess, give it to me."

Reports piled up, a dirty truth. Hints of trouble had slipped through, vague nudges lost in the daily blah. Paul seethed inside, exploding like a dull thud, defeated. They'd had solids, just no way to tie them up in time.

A female analyst pushed through, handing him a file. "Sir, this," timid but sure, eyes covering all of him.

Paul read fast, tapping the corner. "Where'd you find this?"

"Old intercept, sir. Almost passed it by," she said, close enough to smell him.

The page blurred into focus— "second wave," "sleeping giant." More coming, worse? Paul's thoughts connecting it all, old instincts kicking. "Get Strohm," he said. "Keep this here until, we're sure."

She ran away, and Paul just stood there, all alone, cold, and surrounded by shadows he didn't recognize.

September 12th 9:15 a.m. -Washington D.C.

Across town, Brian Strohm watched the President's worried face on a screen, surrounded by security. "Everything changes, gentlemen," the President declared. "Who is the mastermind behind this?"

Brian's shoulders rose, hands flexing from habit. "Mr. President, Al-Qaeda's the call so far, still checking. We act fast, careful, no room for error."

Brian added with a sigh. "Mr. President," he said, stammering, "word also just came—might be more on the way."

The President's eyes laser on him. "Tell me."

Brian spelled it out, the words measured and deliberate, hinting at more than he was saying. September 11th might be just the start of it all.

September 12th 7:30 p.m. -Washington D.C.

Paul spent the late hours navigating various agencies, cajoling, prompting, and even begging for their collective cooperation. Old rivalries were strong, with each side fiercely protecting what was theirs.

"Listen," he commanded, his voice silencing the grumbling, shifting, eye-rolling agency heads. "Your rules and territory are familiar to me."

They kept agreeing with him, even though they probably didn't mean it. Paul felt the resistance; years of habit were hard to break. Could he fix this mess?

September 15th 8:00 a.m. -Washington D.C.

Some days later, Paul found himself in a confidential meeting with Strohm and selected high-ranking individuals. Day's weight silenced the space. Strohm stopped the meeting after twenty minutes for some stretching, the precise way he rolled his shoulders and popped his back, irritating Paul. Everyone looked at each other, but Paul stayed quiet, picking up on the guy's strange, too-controlled tics—something felt wrong, it rubbed him the wrong way.

"Keogh," Strohm said, stepping out of a stretch, "how's the intel flow?"

Paul carefully picked words. "Sir, we're moving, but it's slow. The walls between us run muddy, not just systems, but people too stubborn."

Strohm's eyes held, thinking. "And the quiet projects? The off books?"

Everyone went quiet, wanting to hear more. Paul knew he was talking about super advanced, black-ops tech that most of these guys couldn't understand. "That's a hard one, sir," he said. "They're locked for a reason but we might have to peek inside."

Suddenly they were all thinking about secret labs and wild tech. No one said much, but Paul caught the shift—each man chasing his own guess about what hid behind those locked doors.

# Six

## *Breadcrumbs*

Paul stands before his office wall, a sprawl of photos, documents, and red string stretching across it. Two weeks have passed since the attacks, yet he feels no closer to grasping how they missed such a massive threat. The hijackers' photos stare back, their eyes taunting his every move. He rubs his face, dark rings marking sleepless nights. A half-empty cup of coffee sits on his desk, hemmed by flight school records and visa applications. He scans the documents again, a detail catching his attention.

"How do we miss this?" he mutters to himself, leaning in, his own voice echoing in his head. *Come on, Paul, you should've seen it,* he thinks, one hand rubbing his forehead, lost in the mess of how this slipped by.

A competent official spots the glaring holes in one hijacker's visa application right away. Empty fields and odd answers beg for a hard look, but it passes anyway. Paul frowns, his mind arguing back at him. *This isn't right. How did this even get approved?* He flips through the others, hands moving fast, spotting the same lazy gaps in visa files, flight logs, and scattered agency notes piling up. *Not just Florida, look at all this. What's wrong with us? These outfits never talk. We sat on gold and let it rot.*

He sifts through the stack, a memory hitting hard. He stumbles back, staring at the paper in his hand, then kicks the desk's leg, wincing as his toe throbs. "Oh crap," he says aloud, then scolds himself, *you knew something felt off back then. Why didn't you push?*

Ticked, he digs through old reports, pulling one from months ago, middle eastern men at a Florida flight school. He stares at his own notes, brushing it off as quirks. *You filed it, Paul,* his mind yells, *and let it sit. Look at this, jet training, cash, no confirmations.* He shakes his head, "How can I be so blind?" *You had it right there,* his thoughts shout back, *and you walked away.*

The men zeroed in on steering big planes, skipping takeoffs and landings. They dodged questions, paid cash, and stayed quiet. Every clue screamed for notice, and he shrugged it off. *What were you thinking?* he asks himself, hands gripping his hair. *This wasn't some hunch to ignore. You should've dug more.*

Paul was now irritated with himself, his mistake pounding him. *Could I have stopped this?* he wondered, repeating in his skull. *A little more pushback, and maybe they're alive.* Images fade in, victims' faces, towers burning, families sobbing, each stab he feels deep. *You let it slide, Paul. You.*

Anger at himself gets the better of him. *No fixing yesterday,* he tells himself, kicking the desk's leg again and cursing under his breath, *but I won't let it happen again. This mess drives me now.* He sets his mind to chase the truth, wherever it leads.

A knock at the door. Brian Strohm enters.

"Keogh, what do you have?" he asks.

Paul his conscience heavy. He pauses to clear his throat. "Sir, we've found a mess of slip-ups. The visa system let us down badly. These guys," he points to their photos, "should not have entered the country. The warning signs stick out plain as day, but nobody caught them or cared." He pauses again. "And sir, I made a serious mistake. Months ago, I filed a report about strange stuff at a flight school in Florida, middle eastern men training only on big planes, skipping takeoffs and landings. I figured no one would take it seriously, so I didn't push it."

Brian smirks, his tone dripping with disdain. "How? How do you let this happen right under your nose, Keogh?"

Embarrassed, Paul responded. "I don't know yet, sir. But I plan to find out. I blame myself for my mistake, but I think this goes beyond one slip. I'll make sure this gets handled."

Brian stares at him with disgust as he leaves the room. "Do it, Keogh. We cannot afford to make more mistakes. Update me on every step."

Paul remembers a mission in the middle east, the details coming back to him.


Early 1999 - Undisclosed Location, Afghanistan

Paul Keogh adjusts his local garb, the hidden documents pressing against his chest. He gathers this intel over months of grueling work, detailed plans of Al-Qaeda's opium smuggling routes funding their operations across the middle east. He knows if he delivers it to Langley, it might choke the terrorist group's cash flow and stop attacks brewing in the region. His earpiece crackles. "Horseman, this is Eagle Eye. Status report."

Paul sweeping the dusty streets around him. "Eagle Eye, Horseman here. I head to rendezvous. Package stays secure."

"Copy that, Horseman. Watch yourself. We spotted movements near the compound. Move careful."

He spends months building sources, stitching together info. This intel he carries holds lives in the balance, but he needs to reach the extraction point. A respected linguist sharp in Saudi Arabian and Farsi, he takes this solo mission after others stumble. He navigates the narrow, winding streets of the small village an hour early for pickup, and stops at a market coffee shop to blend in. Sipping his coffee, he overhears two men whispering in Farsi around the corner, their words freezing him in place.

"The Sheikh feels pleased," Khalid says. "The Americans chase shadows while we grow strong. Soon, we strike at the heart of their arrogance."

The other man chuckles. "Yes, and they suspect nothing. The plan moves ahead. Our brothers in the west say flight training goes unnoticed."

Paul tensed up at those words. Flight training in the west? That's not in his intelligence reports. However, the mention of airplanes catches his attention. Years of experience tracking threats to American airspace—a skill that has led to jobs detecting those who would use U.S. assets against the country—heighten his awareness. He knows they're referring to Osama Bin Laden, a prominent figure in intelligence circles. The operatives keep talking, dropping fragments that sink into him, talk of a "grand plan," of bringing "the west" down, of a "day that would shake the world." The words sound bold, almost crazy, and Paul brushes them off in his head, *have these guys lost it? This sounds mad.*

Paul wrestles inside. Does he stay to hear more? His extraction team waits, the opium routes intel vital in his pocket. Yet this new talk points to something odd, though he doubts its importance now. Footsteps approach before he settles it. He slips away quietly, heart thumping, and heads to the pickup. He resolves to add this to his report, knowing the intelligence world's hard truth, without proof and agency teamwork, it risks fading into the paper stacks. He writes it down anyway.

The helicopter lifts off, pulling him to safety. Paul thinks over what he heard, the note lodged in his brain for later, if he finds time to dig into it. He slumped in his seat, relieved; this was just another extraction in a long career nearing its end. He's looking forward to settling down and avoiding close calls.

Present Day -Washington D.C.

Paul Keogh pulls back to the present, a new drive running through him. He spots the clues now, clear as day, sitting there all along. The intelligence community's refusal to share, the mess of bureaucratic delays, the overlooked links all pile up to 9/11's ruin.

He calls the one person he trusts to tie this mess together. "This is Keogh. Get me all you have on Osama Bin Laden's time in Afghanistan during the Soviet Afghan War. Thanks."

He sets the phone down, purpose lifting him. He senses he's on to something major, a lead that might flip how they see everything before 9/11.

For the next few days, Paul was knee-deep in old files and intel reports. A story unfolds, pulling him in and rattling him all at once.

Osama Bin Laden shifts from a partner against Soviet troops to a planner hating the west with every breath. Paul follows his trail, a rich Saudi kid hardening into a mujahideen fighter, then rising as terror's architect.

"He turns our own moves against us," Paul mutters, linking Bin Laden's tricks. The training, the equipment, the strategy all traces back to CIA plays from the Cold War days.

Paul broke down the fallout. Hints of strange tech in buried files, ones he studied with Amy Rockwell and Brian Strohm on yesterday's video call, rubs wrong against what he recalls of that era's tools. He wonders if this hooks into today's trouble, if he's missing something right in front of him.

Before he chases that thought, his office door swings wide open and an assistant bursts in. "A lead. A flight school instructor in Florida, not the one you met, but a guy who quit months back, stepped up now. He overheard some students talking plans about planes, says local authorities ignored him when he warned them something wasn't right."

Paul hoped that this would crack it wide open. "Pull everything on this instructor, what he hears, what he tells them, who brushes him off. Book me a flight to Florida. I'll meet him myself. I need to know he's not wasting my time with this."

The assistant races out. Paul faces his wall of evidence again. He feels a web growing, one bigger than most dare to guess. The crumbs lie there, spread over the years and places, and he needs to track them down.

He knows there is danger up ahead. Powerful players are secretly working to keep these connections hidden. From his desk, Paul retrieves an old file containing a sketch of a gold triangle—its points circled and labeled "Trinity"—a word from prior notes that continues to bother him. Examining it from every angle, he's captivated by its mysterious allure, sensing hidden meaning. 9/11, Bin Laden, tech whispers, and the trinity are interconnected. He's committed to solving it.

# Seven

## *Black Projects*

Larry reached for his ruined uniform in the cold firehouse. Smoke and dust cover every inch of it, tugging him back to Ground Zero's hell with every whiff. He puts off this task for days, avoiding the flood of grief it causes, the faces of those he couldn't save still visiting him. He leans against the locker, worn out, aching to bring closure to families who cling to hope even now.

He digs into the pockets, catching something sharp. He pulls out the small, metallic object, and examines it.

"What the," Larry says marveling at its brilliant shine.

He sits back on the bench and recalls finding it. Back in those first hours at Ground Zero, he spotted this thing, a flat, glowing piece, among the piles of rubble. He figured it was a shard from some office machine or maybe a plane fragment. He zipped it into his pocket, secured it tight, planning to check it later, but his head stayed fixed on finding people, pulling anyone he could from the debris. Now, weeks later, with the locker room empty, lights dim, and no more people to find, he pulls it out.

The device's surface catches the light in a way he can't make sense of. Three beams radiate, bending it into something almost alive, like a box fighting to form. He squints at it, hesitant, watching blurry shapes across its sides, towers, maybe, or just shadows he can't make out. A warm, barely audible buzz in his palm leaves him stumped, his head shaking in disbelief. This flat piece shifts, stretching beyond itself, like it doesn't belong here. He needs to tell someone, but no one is there, nerves jumping, yet he can't peel his eyes off its living glow.

Phone in hand, "Chief? It's Evans. I found something at Ground Zero. You need to see this."

He explains it, hearing the chief's demeanor turning into something serious. Within minutes, they settle on handing it to the FBI for a look.

Larry sits, torn between grief for the fallen and the item he clutches. The past two weeks were rough on him. He found a kid in the rubble who wasn't moving, eyes empty. It affected him more than any other adult he had to rescue. He wished he could have saved the kid, wished he could have warned his parents to keep him home from daycare. No survivors, only ghosts and recovery. He feels this strange triangle connects to that day and he hopes it helps, even if peace stays out of reach for him.

September 26th 8:45 a.m. -Venice, Florida

On the plane, engine noise calmed Keogh. He's revisiting Florida's flight school to investigate missed 9/11 clues.

Seeing Tampa, Paul remembers his last visit. He shrugged off concerns from local contacts, chalking it up to nerves or prejudice. He's kicking himself over all the little things he missed before the disaster. No more missed clues!

Venice rolls into sight. Tourists wander, locals carry on, everything looking ordinary. He struggled to wrap his head around this sleepy coastal town sheltering some of history's worst terrorists.

There's Jefferson Aviation flight school, just like last time. This time, Paul didn't miss a thing, his eyes caught all the action.

Noticing Paul through the office window, Alan Beckers went outside, their handshake weak. Paul notes the man's weariness—visible in his sunken eyes and shaky hands, which Paul suspects is due to heavy drinking—but refrains from judgment, understanding the toll of 9/11. The analyst's note Paul found said the ex-chief instructor quit. Too many new Middle Eastern students, who were rude and barely spoke English. He'd had enough.

"Let's hang out here," Beckers said. Those folks inside are fed up with reporters harassing them.

Paul agreed, then went to the next page, "Okay, my team's findings are..."

"Mr. Keogh," Beckers says. "I keep running it over in my head, how many times I missed it. If I'd just..."

Paul stops him. "We're all kicking ourselves, Mr. Beckers. I'm here to catch what we didn't. Walk me through it again, every bit, even what may seem small."

Beckers lays out the hijackers' time at the school, and Paul picks up hints he overlooked before. They zeroed in on flying big planes, skipped takeoffs and landings, dodged questions about who they were. They paid cash up front, kept to themselves, all the details he'd shrugged off then, but now, with hindsight, they ate at him, hints he might have acted on if he'd caught them sooner.

Becker paused, looking this way and that, and Paul braced himself, waiting. He puts a hand on Becker's shoulder, stares him down, and asks, "What's up?" Beckers sobbed. I didn't mention it earlier because it sounds unbelievable and might make me seem crazy.

Paul comforted him with a reminder. "This matters."

Becker blurted something out. "Other men showed up sometimes, not the middle eastern guys, but these ones in black suits, waiting in a tinted SUV. The hijackers met them, but it's weird. They didn't talk, they just stood there, staring."

Paul thinks this clicks with tales of men in black he's heard in the field, not some conspiracy stuff, but real talk he trusts, and now Beckers hands him the same info. "Did you ever see these men in black, up close?"

Beckers gave a shrug. "Nah, they made sure to keep their hats low and faces hidden. But once," he stops, then pushes on, "I caught one passing something to a hijacker. It was pointed, metal, shiny a little. I assumed they were covering the lesson costs since I never knew who funded them. I didn't ask to avoid trouble with the owner, who was pleased with the profits. It sounds odd, but it's true."

Paul pictures that sketch in his head, a gold triangle with three points called Trinity. This ties in. He scribbles a note to cross-check with Amy and Brian back in Washington.

Again, his hand finds its way to Beckers' shoulder. "You did right by coming forward, Alan. This helps, you're not crazy. Keep an eye out for anything else out of the ordinary, and thanks for your time. It's gonna be okay, we'll sort this out, make sure it doesn't happen again. I appreciate you stepping up." Stepping back, he realized that something far more sinister than terrorism was afoot. More profound than planes hitting towers, a field, the Pentagon.

Hungry from too much coffee and no food, Paul pulls into the local diner, a frequent haunt of the hijackers. He needs to refuel to finish his work and organize his notes before returning to Washington. He's found that chatting with locals often helps him find leads, so he's hoping to get some gold here. He slides into a booth, and veteran waitress Marge is right there. "You're visiting, huh?", she said, pouring the coffee, real sassy. "You don't blend in here, you look like a big shot."

Paul remains polite despite her nosy edge. "I'm checking on some middle eastern guys who trained at the flight school down the street. They ate here a lot. You ever see them, notice anything off?"

Marge lights up, leaning in with a gossip's dream. "Oh, something sticks with me, I brushed it off then. Those fellas, when they left, I swear they vanished into thin air, stepped around the corner and poof, gone, like magic. No car, nothing. Once, I think I saw one chatting with a suit, fella missing two fingers on his hand, sunglasses hiding his face. They'd pop up from nowhere, then vanish again. Sounds loony, don't it?"

Paul sits back, glad her gossip hit his table. "Not as loony as you'd think, Marge. Thanks." He downs his coffee, leaves a fat tip on the table, grateful for the lead.

He exits the Diner, the clues are forming a picture, a picture he's unsure he wants to see.

September 26<sup>th</sup> 4:45 p.m. -Washington D.C.

Amy reviewed files on the screen. She wasn't just looking for data, she was on a hunt for it, and she felt a pattern forming. Her brownish-red hair came down from the bun, making her stand out in this plain space, with sharp cheekbones and green eyes that highlight her beauty. Her elegant appearance suggests a gala, not NSA work, yet she excels there, fully immersed, prioritizing her sharp intellect and pursuit of answers. She makes connections others don't see.

She pulls up reports from the late 1990s, Clinton years, and scans them close, a string of anonymous messages that stumped the agencies back then. She flips through scribble, spotting coded lines, redacted, cryptic, like Nostradamus quatrains she's seen lately, a style no one decoded in time.

She suspected Bin Laden was behind the cryptic warnings.

They attributed the simultaneous, untraceable signals from various locations to either hacking or a system malfunction. The memory of September 11th was still vivid as she scrolled through files and found a sketch—a gold triangle. She stops and looks at it, recognizing something she's seen in these folders before, always dismissed as some crazy person's rant. She's not sure what it means, but she'll check it out later.

She composed the message to Paul, outlined her discovery, and sent it. The more she thought about it, the more certain she became, this wasn't just a clue to what was coming. It was the beginning of understanding what had already happened.

A knock cuts her off. Brian Strohm strides in. "Rockwell, we've got something. The FBI sent over a device a firefighter pulled from Ground Zero. Let's go, move it." He waves a hand, rude and dismissive, pushing her along.

Amy jumps at his bark, trailing behind him to a secure lab, sensing his sour mood. A familiar triangle, like a warped motherboard, sits on a long white table, the piece Larry Evans found. Alive, the tech pulsed warmly, reacting to her stare. Her mouth drops. That's the triangle from the sketch.

"Well, what is it?" Brian demands, testing her.

Amy starts to speak, agitation showing as Brian hovers, rushing her. Her beauty softens his bite. She likes to mull things slowly, methodically, not spit out guesses, but he doesn't get that, without working with her daily. "I'm not sure, sir," she says, afraid of her own words. "But I bet it ties to what made September 11th happen."

She started poking at it when Paul walked in, back from Florida, with notes alongside, itching to spill what he'd got. A guard swung the lab door wide, two more posted outside, letting him through after Brian's heads-up to meet here. He walks in and finds them analyzing a device. One look, and he knows it matches what Beckers saw, that sketch burned in his mind.

"Where'd you get that?" Paul demands an answer.

Brian fills him in on Larry Evans' find, a joking undertone slipping through his flat words, making light of it. Paul shoots him a look, figuring he's clocked too many days without sleep. Paul runs through his Florida haul, and the three wonder where to turn next, the stakes just rose.

"We need to get access to these black projects," Paul says, keeping it quiet. "Something's up here, we've got to look at this different."

With eyes glued to the object, Amy and Paul sensed an imminent revelation; Brian, however, merely smirked, leaving them to wonder what he knew that they didn't.

Paul's phone goes off, an unknown number. He picks up. "Hello?"

"Mr. Keogh," a synthesized voice cuts in—eerie and clipped like it's pieced together. "We know about that device you're studying. Meet us at the Lincoln Memorial, midnight, if you want the truth."

As the call abruptly ended, Paul was left staring at his phone, unable to speak. He looked at Brian and Amy, a confused look on his face. Midnight, Lincoln Memorial, we're meeting up. Amy bit her lip, Brian rolled his eyes, but Paul stuck to his guns. "I'm off to set up a backup, everything will be fine."

Suspense builds in the Pentagon lab as they wait.

September 26th 5:45 p.m. -Afghanistan

From his makeshift shelter atop a ridge, Farid has gathered wood for warmth and comfort. Dry riverbeds carved paths through the dusty landscape, snaking between the sharp, brown mountains that rose around him. His shelter perches clever and low, a trick he masters over years, one the other men admire him for. A knack that keeps him alive while he works Paul's side under their noses. Every shift in movement on the rocky slopes was caught by his watchful eye. Blinded by the sun's reflection on the stone during the day and threatened by hidden dangers in the night, he sleeps little, catching only short rests when the wind subsides.

His radio sits close, spitting bursts of talk from the men he blends with. Al-Qaeda voices he pretends to follow. He turns it down, sifting their words for meaning, tuned in from years of listening through noise.

He serves as Paul's eyes and ears in this barren stretch, slipping him secrets for years while playing the loyal local. He moves carefully, keeps his habits tight, no sudden shifts, no loose talk, his routine ways shielding him from suspicion. Pride swells in him, not loud, but sure. He must pull this off without a slip, his cover a shield for something higher than himself.

As the sun drops below the mountains, the sky glows red over the village. People sometimes gather to watch a small break in their hard lives. Farid stuffs his radio in his bag, hoping for a quiet night, but then, crackle!—a voice. He ripped open the pack, grabbed it, and held it to his ear, barely breathing so he could hear.

The data forms a familiar code, a rhythm from his training, reminiscent of Nostradamus's riddles. Bin Laden favored them for top-secret missions. With years of practice, Farid rapidly uncovers the meaning, a dark and monstrous plan is revealed, dwarfing the impact of September 11th.

Farid pulls his secure comms, American technology entrusted to him by Paul, from a hidden compartment within a battered, untouched Koran.

He cherishes the tool, a symbol of his significance, its concealment protecting him from discovery. He flips it on, this call matters. He let Paul know there was a threat, hoping to prevent something bad. His cautious life plays a role in that fight.

September 26th 6:45 p.m. -Washington D.C.

The rain-slick Lincoln Memorial steps felt like a bad omen to Paul Keogh as he trudged upward, nearing midnight, and he almost turned back. He tucked his hands into his coat pockets, touching the folded notes from Florida, Beckers' words, that sketch of the gold triangle, helps him feel safe even if in his mind. Lincoln's statue high above, its stone bulk catching the faint glow of floodlights, a white giant peering over the mall's dark sprawl. Paul wonders if this meeting is a trap or a lifeline.

On the cold platform, he paced, the sound of his heels on marble punctuated by his breath, which plumed white into the air. Replay of the call's voice fuels his paranoia about those who know about Larry's find. *What do they have on it? Do they tie to the suits Beckers saw?* He stops, leans on a pillar, puts his hand in his pocket, feeling comfort under his thumb, taking a chance on trust that he's not sure will pay off.

You could hear the footsteps... crisp, together, drumming off the columns. Paul spotted two things cutting through the park as he looked around in the dark. They sharpened their outlines, tall and lean in matching suits. Consistent with Becker's description. He stood taller, fists clenched.

Paul heard the smooth, unfamiliar voice again on the phone, saying, "Mr. Keogh." He gave a brief nod and a tip of the hat. "Glad you made it!"

Paul's chin snapped up, he spoke calmly, forcing the words out. "You claimed you've got something on the device. Let's hear it."

Stepping up, the one's face was cut by silver light from his hat. "Not here," he warned. "Come with us." With his suit flapping in the wind, he turns, puts a hand to his hat, and descends the steps.

Paul trails them, feeling like he can't keep down his last meal. These two moved with an unsettling precision, their actions too flawless, too robotic, as if controlled by a distant, unseen operator. He wonders if he's walking into a setup he won't walk out of.

Halting near the memorial, they observed the dark, still water of the reflecting pool mirroring the memorial's light. The entity shifts. "That device is going to change everything."

Paul stops. "Spell it out. Who are you?"

The suits turn slow and deliberate. "We serve interests outside your world's grasp, Mr. Keogh."

"That's no damn answer," Paul fires back, he plants his feet wider, ready to fight his way out.

Sensing tension, it responds "We're laying out a truth that'll flip your take on the last few years. You up for that smart guy?"

Paul was not having this. "Give me the real stuff. No more games. Now."

"Alright," he said, approaching. "That tech you've got shouldn't be here. It's from a future that got derailed."

Paul latching onto the words. "Future? You talking time travel?"

The sarcastic one adds. "Not like that. Picture it as borrowed knowledge, robbed by rogue outfits chasing power." He let Paul absorb what he'd said. "Were you ever curious about the precision of the plane impacts?"

"Do you mean September 11th?" Paul spits, his hands relaxing as if to grab the info.

"Ran on tech your people can't touch yet," the one shares. "Remote systems locked the controls, cut the pilots out cold, nailed every target, straight from this borrowed stash. Our gear hooked the terrorists into the planes, mind-to-machine, no breaking it." He pulls a slim, metallic rod from his coat, its surface a perfect gold, pulsing dim. "This runs it. Only two exist, we hold one, the other got stolen."

Paul stares at the rod. That triangle sketch flashes in his head. "Why drag me into this?"

Their eyes met briefly. "You have a chance to fix this, Mr. Keogh."

With Paul so still, the speaker's words about the terror war hit harder. It was a giant, complicated problem beyond anyone's grasp, making regular folks vulnerable. He adjusted his weight, the rustle of his coat a backdrop to his mental image of Amy, Brian, and the triangle back at the lab. It's more than planes and towers now.

"Who are you, straight up?" Paul demands.

His hat falls, revealing a flawless face with unsettling eyes. He said, seriously, "We're architects; we design the future." Mr. Keogh, you need to defend your world, there's a threat you don't even know about."

Paul legs giving way, as they vanished. Moving into his pockets, he grounded himself as darkness closed in.

September 26th 7:00 p.m. -Washington D. C.

Back pain told Amy how long she'd been sitting. Although the triangle on the table was static, it hadn't stabilized. Calibration failed; it reacted against all she knew of structure and energy. She went for it once more. Cold and still but more alive than the detached human sitting with her.

"Brian," she says loud, hoping to revive him, catching the edge of fear and wonder. "I've got something here. You're not going to believe this."

Brian Strohm brushes by her shoulder, as he peers at the device. The triangle shimmers, then spits out a holographic projection, light beams spilling across the table. Images swirl in the glow, planes slicing into towers on September 11th, TWA Flight 800 bursting midair, even murky scenes they can't place, all playing side by side. He was amazed.

"This is wild," Brian mutters. "Time tech? Time Travel? Space Manipulation? Is that what we're looking at?"

"Take a look," Amy said, pressing the side of the triangle. Numbers scrolled across a glowing light, same as those from old intercepts she'd cracked. Her eyes were glued to Brian, not the display. Touching it made it feel more real than the reports ever did.

Since joining Brian's team, Amy has relentlessly pursued his approval, using his ambition as a benchmark for her own self-worth. He glanced back, giving her the once-over. Her eagerness grossed him out. She looked like a needy beggar, not the tough, competent woman she was. "Good job, Rockwell, but don't get ahead of yourself—lots of others could've solved that," he scoffed, turning away and ignoring her completely. Pride filled Amy, even though he despised her; his eyes burned into her.

Her computer beeped, breaking the quiet. This email pops up from nowhere, the subject: "The Truth About Flight 800 and ValuJet 592" (in HUGE letters). She clicks it open, eyes scanning the text, each line rewriting everything she thought she knew.

# Eight

## *Men In Black*

Paul descends the Lincoln Memorial steps, cursing the wind and the architects' words. He reaches into his pockets, feeling his old leather wallet, a favorite for what's in it, a token he holds onto when things get tough, guiding him through hard times. He was off to the Pentagon to fill Amy and Brian in on the stolen golden rod, its power was a serious threat. A watcher is present on Washington's quiet streets.

Paul checks his cracked watch, then feels a shift. He stumbled, then he found himself sitting down on a bench in a strange pod, all the blurry city lights outside.

"Mr. Keogh," a voice booms, coming from everywhere yet nowhere, calm and familiar like it's stitched into the space. "Listen close, this matters. Your world faces ruin, and discernment may yet help your people."

The walls of the pod slide back, Paul stands up wobbly, catching his balance as the room opens up into a big chamber, with a high curved ceiling, the air quiet and motionless. Two figures beside him look completely at ease; they're as tall as the Architects but stiffer, in those dull silver suits, with faces that are too perfect and eyes like stone.

"The Council sent us," the left one said. "What you heard tonight is only the start. The golden triangle called Trinity, and the golden rod that commands it, holds power beyond human knowledge. Someone stole that rod, and now your world's breaking apart."

The right one steps up, hands at its waist. "Our rogue brotherhood stole that rod, planned the attacks on your America, those planes guided by its force." Paul's head overloads, going from one idea to the next. The golden rod's power flashing in his mind, the only anchor keeping him from drifting out of himself.

"You stand at a turning point," the figure says. "Keep this to yourself. Unleashed too soon, it would tear your world apart."

Paul loses balance. For a second, he isn't sure if it's the floor or his own conviction that slipped. The room holds, but something in him doesn't.

He blinks, the warped space around him gone, and he's back on the street, the damp grass at the curb a reassuring touch against his hands. He checked his watch; time stood still. The gold light vanished, leaving him stunned.

A black SUV pulls up, its tires gripping the wet street, as Paul struggles to get up slowly, temporarily blinded by a man in a suit stepping out, his badge reflecting under a streetlamp. "Mr. Keogh? It's security detail. You, okay? Thought we caught an anomaly on the feed, probably static." His eyes, probing.

Paul straightens, the Council's warning, a load he can't get rid of. He slides into the SUV, safety feeling good, wrestling with what to spill to Amy and Brian, Trinity, rogues, a turning point, and what to keep to himself. The world's fate rests on his next words. A difficult decision holds him at the door, his knuckles whitening as he grips the handle.

September 26$^{th}$ 7:15 p.m. -Afghanistan

Farid sits cross-legged in the cave, the September night's dry air cool against his jacket as he moves the secure device to his ear, finally tapping into Osama's channel. He scribbles notes about their next move from the line he's cracked, pencil scratching fast, hoping the blunt tip holds out. The connection, usually clean, fills with static, and he listens close, tongue resting loose against his teeth, straining to catch every word, small voices threading through, electric and warped, not human.

He ends the transmission, thumb pressing the switch down. His nerves fall out telling him something's off, the hairs on his neck lifting. He turns slow, careful not to make a noise, his heart beating against his ribs like a trapped bird, eyes blind to the dark.

A figure stands there, its silhouette long against the cave's open mouth under the Afghan night. Farid turns more, facing where he feels the presence is pulling, undeniable and strange.

"Hello, Farid," it says, a voice bypassing his ears, sliding straight into his thoughts like a stone dropping into deep water. "We need to talk about your planet's future."

September 26<sup>th</sup> 7:40 p.m. -Washington D.C.

Paul Keogh almost at the Pentagon, sliding his wedding ring off his finger and pocketing it, pushing it deep into the corner to keep it safe, a move to keep focus, married to his work now that his divorce is done. The Council's words stay with him, that golden rod and triangle called Trinity—stolen by the rogue brotherhood, ripping the world loose. Paul thinks on its name—Trinity—a sacred symbol from his Catholic roots, etched from boyhood Sundays, wondering if it's more than tech, something supernatural seeping through what they put into his mind back in that pod.

Brian, as Secretary of Defense, had tapped Paul before September 11th, valuing his diplomatic way of linking CIA and NSA, a liaison smoothing year of silos. Paul runs this task force now, a crew of top agents in a sealed section Brian set up. He pauses at the retinal scanner, brushing by the biometric pad, rehearsing in his head what to share and what to hold back.

A guard lets him through after the scanner blinks green, one of the regulars who knows Paul's face, high clearance clicking into place. Paul is torn between revealing the stakes set by those strange beings or keeping them a secret. Should he take the risk or play it safe? Amy is loyal. Her trust is a lifeline he's counted on, but Brian's attitude lately, less cooperative since the attacks, bothers him. He decides mid-step, share a piece, not the whole crazy pile, not yet.

Paul steps in. "Amy, Brian, we need to talk," he says, clearing his voice, then adds, "What do you have?" Amy glances up fast, while Brian stands up, present but off somehow, his join-in half-hearted. Paul lays out the

Lincoln Memorial meet, strange figures, wild tech, keeping it sane, his calm cracking just enough to hint at the madness he holds back.

Strategy is finalized. Paul and Amy communicate silently with a look, both on the same page, while Brian shows no interest, a bit odd to Paul but he puts it out of his mind for now. Frozen, Amy pauses, Brian shrugs, and all three are confronted with a truth too wild to process, they wonder if they should persevere or quit, their limits severely stretched.

# Nine
## *Echoes*

Paul shifts in his chair, back stiff from weeks in this cluttered office, files stacked high on every surface. A pile of cold coffee takes over a desk. Food boxes from the cafeteria litter the floor, grease stains marking their endless nights. He catches himself looking Amy, her face caught in the windows' light, dark circles hollowing her eyes, matching his own exhaustion.

Paul, deep in thought, the Lincoln Memorial meeting with those beings still bothering him, words about stolen tech. He watches Amy, her glasses smudged with grime from days without a break and wonders how she even sees through the lenses. How much can he tell her? How much stays inside?

"Paul, check this," Amy says. She points at her computer, a redacted Eisenhower-era document under her cursor.

Paul reads the patchy text. "What's this?"

Amy whispered, despite the room being soundproof. "A 1954 report. Eisenhower vanished for five days. They claimed a dental trip but look." She taps a less hidden line. "Colorado, New Mexico, meetings with 'foreign delegates.'"

Paul sits up. "You mean..."

With a serious shake of her head, Amy showed she meant business. "Eisenhower met aliens more than once." She pulls up more files, spreading them across the monitors. "Texas, Colorado, New Mexico, all through his term, UFO hotspots every time."

Paul asks, "What else?"

"It's more," Amy says, still hushed. "JFK too. Nixon obsessed over it." She holds up a manilla file. "This one says Nixon took Jackie Gleason to a Florida base to see alien ships."

"Jackie Gleason? The Honeymooners guy?" Paul asks, half-laughing.

"He chased UFO stories," Amy explains, flipping pages. She adds "Not just presidents, though. The '60s files say aliens walked D.C. streets, spending time with Congress, top officials, with no fuss about it."

Paul sinks back. "Decades of this. What did they want?"

"Here's the kicker," Amy says, fanning papers. "These files say the aliens pushed against war, hated nukes, wanted our leaders to ease off conflict."

Paul sits, thinking of that triangle from the 9/11 wreckage, wondering if she will know the answer. "Then how'd their tech land with terrorists?"

Amy digs through her stack. "No idea yet. But this alien trail ties to September 11th. I'd bet on it, along with the Trinity and those beings you met."

Paul thinks of those suited guys, things, whatever, at the memorial, their hints of old government ties clicking with these pages. "What 'foreign delegates' yank a president off the grid for days?"

Amy in sync with him. "The kind we're not meant to clock," she says. "Paul, these files connect somehow. I've mapped data for years, pieced patterns no one else sees, and I'm telling you, it's all adding up."

The door swung open, and she got cut off. Brian Strohm shows up, looking worried, something else in his eyes. "How's it going?" he asks, expecting answers, not more waiting on them.

"Sir," Amy starts, "we've dug up historical context. Paul needs the full picture now."

Brian cuts in, "Agreed. Paul, this stays here. Clear?"

Paul throws his hands up, half-exasperated. "What more is there?"

"There are programs," Brian his tone serious, "black projects so deep even intel barely knows them. Technology and entities the public can't handle."

Paul lifts an eyebrow. "Entities? Like the ones I saw the other night. How many are we talking?"

Brian pauses. "We're not alone, Paul. Haven't been for ages. Parts of the government have dealt with aliens since way back, kept it undercover."

This lands heavy, Brian's words hitting hard. Paul feels confirmed, proof he's not losing it, those Lincoln Memorial beings real, not some wild dream he cooked up.

"There's more," Brian adds, crossing to a vault in the wall. He punches in codes, the locker popping open with a pop and a click. He lifts out a sleek black case, pulling two devices like VR headsets from inside.

"These," he says, holding them up, "are reverse engineered from top alien technology. They dial into frequencies that only these glasses can reach, years of work creating them, to show reality as it is." Brian, annoyed at being teacher, his ego itching to skip this chore and focus on himself, planning in the back of his mind to keep them busy, he adds, "It took decades to match the timing, layer the signals just right."

Paul recalling the memorial's "borrowed knowledge" line, tech beyond them. He takes one device, delicately and looks at its features.

"Brace yourselves," Brian warns.

Paul and Amy putting the devices on, cautious—*are we good?* —before sliding them over their heads. Nothing at first, then the room goes on full tilt. Visible wavelengths burst; thoughts, feelings form visible shapes.

Paul stared, speechless.

He turns to Brian and Amy, seeing them in a new way. Brian's presence glows deep blue, red streaks cutting through, a mix Paul senses as strength and burden once the tech kicks in. Amy's shines green, gold threads sparking, her smarts and drive clear as the device decodes it for him.

Paul looks at his hands, colors tracing his skin, a view of himself, overwhelming, beautiful, terrifying all at once.

"This is unreal," Amy shares. "I'd been told about this, but wearing it is another level."

"Now you get why we guard this so carefully." Brian says. "It shows people true, and that's not always good to let out."

Paul is amused, the device pulling up history. "This shows the real past," Brian adds, "not the stuff from schoolbooks. Truth we've buried, filling gaps you'll see." Alien outposts sit under Arizona sand, Antarctic ice, ocean depths. Submarines break Arctic ice, watching hidden hubs. Leaders ink deals with aliens, treaties sealing tech swaps over decades, America jumping ahead with aircraft and advancements no other country could match.

"The attacks," Paul says. "9/11. Was it..."

Brian shakes his head. "A rogue faction fed terrorists this alien tech. That precision got through our defenses, supernatural stuff the best couldn't stop. You all did your best, Paul, no one could've seen it."

Paul starts to pull off the headset as Brian catches his look, yanking it off for him. "We're done here," Brian says, cutting Paul's experience short. Paul sees some interesting details, almost seeing the true Brian before the device left his hands. It made him want to see more.

Paul and Amy stared at each other, this truth hitting hard. Brian and Amy already know chunks of it, but Paul, with all his years in the field, military, intel, now liaison between agencies, can't believe he wasn't in on this, wondering why they held back 'til now.

Brian cuts in, "We need to use this tech on specific 9/11 leads, nothing more," he commanded.

"The crash sites," Amy says, wanting Brian's approval. "We've combed Flight 93 a dozen times, but with these..."

"Exactly," Brian says, giving her the nod she wants. "I'll set us up for Pennsylvania. Keeps us focused there." Amy stands tall. Validated.

Paul asks, "When?"

"Tomorrow," Brian says. "I'll pull clearance to move these. They're near alien relics themselves, discretion's everything."

Next morning, Paul and Amy sit in a secure briefing room, a tight circle of tech staff and security around them. A gray-haired woman in a lab coat, one they've passed in the halls without knowing her role, stands up front, holding one headset.

She starts, "These high-tech glasses show energy and emotions as colors." She runs through what they might mean. "They also tap your instincts, dialing frequencies to pull out truth, filling in what's missing. These will help the investigation."

She lays out safety rules, warning of the mental kick. Paul excited to have such a tool, elbows on his knees, ready to cut through walls of whatever, this tech a bridge to real facts without the usual runaround.

September 27$^{th}$ 10:50 a.m. -Shanksville, Pennsylvania.

Paul steps out of the government car near Shanksville, the air smelled of fallen leaves and wet soil, a quiet ache settling over the country town. Locals shuffle along the road, heads down under plaid caps, still raw from Flight 93's crash splitting their fields weeks ago. Two FBI agents meet them by the site, one a weathered man with tired eyes, pointing toward the torn earth. "We've scraped every corner here," he says with frustration. "Dead ends pile up. Not much left to say."

Ignoring the agents, Paul winked at Amy. "You've done solid work. Step aside, let us search the area."

The agents pause with respect, recognizing the higher-ups, and back off to clear space. Paul and Amy slip on the high-tech glasses, navigating them solo this time, no guide to lean on. The field comes alive. Brown dirt and green grass burst into wild colors, energy trails weaving through the air, ghosts of that brutal day still present.

Paul walks the site, the glasses painting the agents in curiosity and doubt threading through like sparks. Their boots sinking into the soft earth, they searched beyond the crater's impact, cutting through woods and farmland toward a small pond bathed in afternoon sun.

Amy stops mid-step, her hand lifting to point at a tree line near the water. "There. You see it?"

A subtle light, glimpsed among the overgrown trees, caught Paul's attention, drawing his eyes along her arm. Tiptoeing, hearts pounding, they crunched through leaves till they found it: a little metal thing in the grass, glowing weirdly—but not scary.

Amy says, "What is it?"

"It's like New York." Paul's down on one knee, taking his time to look at it closely. "This one, though, appears operational."

His touch makes the object flash, and they instinctively take a step back. A cube floats into view, projecting a sequence: a plunging plane, a cockpit in chaos, then a blurry but real, non-human shadow. Paul now got it, turning to Amy. "Not aliens aboard, but their tech, their hand. It was here."

A punch to the gut. This isn't just terrorists with alien tools, those beings shaped this attack, touched American soil with intent.

In a quiet moment, Paul stares at the field, visualizing the passengers' fight, the families' losses, and Shanksville's changed streets. His anger is intense, and Amy's usually calm demeanor is starting to crack; you can tell by the way she's holding her notebook.

"We keep this under wraps," Amy says, "If this alien link to 9/11 leaks, it's crazy, panic everywhere."

Paul rubs his thumb and forefinger together nonstop, feeling ticky with nowhere to put it. Fist in air, "We dig further, chase this wherever it goes. For them, the ones lost, their families, we owe them."

The vehicle departed, leaving a trail of dirt in its wake. Paul's all, "What's next?", facing unseen enemies, confusing rules, and ever-increasing risks. It all started with a plane crash, but it's unraveling, and their whole world is changing.

Paul clutched the box to his lap, making sure no one touched it until they were back at the office. The glasses revealed a hidden triangle, a crucial piece of the puzzle. Paul is troubled, he suspects they're being led on a wild goose chase while something important is missed. Bound by the hunt, he and Amy press on, the answers they seek beginning to surface.

# Ten
## *The Unknown*

Paul and Amy sat working late into the night as they had weeks since the 9/11 attacks. It was quiet except for the occasional rustle of papers and the soft footsteps of an assistant, who periodically checked in to refill their coffee or bring supplies. A large cork board dominated one wall, its surface a wall of information. Tape, markers and string interconnected grainy surveillance photos, flight manifests, and handwritten notes, creating a visual map of their investigation. Post-it notes in various colors dotted the board, marking potential leads and unanswered questions. Despite the late hour, both remained laser-focused on their tasks, driven by the need to uncover the truth behind the devastating events that had shaken the nation.

A wall-mounted screen silently cycled through satellite imagery and data streams, while a bank of servers in the corner processed vast amounts of information. The air charged with urgency, a reminder of the critical nature of their work.

Paul rubbed his eyes. His mind kept returning to the strange phone call he'd received earlier that day. The anonymous male caller knew things about the mysterious devices found at Ground Zero and in Pennsylvania, things that weren't in any official report. He glanced at Amy, debating whether to share this information.

"Amy," he said with hesitation, "I received a call today. I don't know who. They... they knew about the devices we found."

"What? How is that possible?" Amy responded.

Paul was tired. "I don't know. But they were talking fast and about things I had a hard time keeping up with and outside of anything we've considered so far."

As if on cue, the phone on Paul's desk rang. He answered it. "Understood. We'll be right there."

Turning to Amy, he said, "That was Brian. He wants to see us."

The walk to the War Room felt longer than usual, every day felt worse and not yet rock bottom. As they moved through the corridors of the Pentagon, Paul reflected on how much had changed in the weeks since the attacks. The nation was still picking itself up, barely, but here, in the heart of America's military complex. The focus had shifted from shock to a relentless pursuit of answers.

When they arrived, they found Brian pacing, his usual composed demeanor noticeably removed. The room, typically full of activity, was quiet, with only the noise of some technological gadget on the table breaking the silence.

"Paul, Amy," he greeted them. "What I'm about to show you doesn't leave this room. Understood?"

They agreed. Brian activated the screen, and a holographic display sprang to life, filling the room with a three-dimensional map of the world. Lit points scattered across various locations, pulsing bright.

"These," Brian said, gesturing to the lights, "alien colonies on Earth."

Paul and Amy stared in silence. The map showed clusters in Arizona, northern Russia, and several underwater locations.

"Alien colonies?" Amy asked.

Brian went on. "For decades, every major world power has been in a race to gain alien technology. The U.S. has stayed ahead, but it's a constant struggle."

He zoomed in on a point in Arizona. "This is one of the largest colonies. We have an... arrangement with them. They observe, and in exchange, we provide resources and protection."

Paul was now about to go out of his mind. How long has this been going on?

Brian sighed. "It goes back further than you'd believe. Eisenhower, JFK, Nixon—they all had direct contact with these beings. There's a top-se-cret organization, run primarily by the CIA and the Space Force, that manages these interactions. It's a very dark black program, completely off the books. Even Congress is in the dark. It is the codeword," panther".

Amy stayed close, studying the map intently. "What about the underwa-ter locations?"

"Ah, yes," Brian said, zooming in on an area off the coast of Virginia Beach. "We've detected significant activity here. The Navy has a special program, using advanced submarines to monitor these sites. The technology is... well, it's unlike anything you've seen before."

He tapped a few commands, and a detailed schematic of a submarine appeared. It looked like nothing like conventional designs and what appeared to be an energy field surrounding it.

"These subs can operate at depth and pressures that would crush normal vessels," Brian explained. "They're equipped with sensors that can detect anomalies in spacetime itself. We've recorded many instances of UFO activity in this area, often emerging from or disappearing into the ocean."

As Brian continued, Paul's thoughts drifted to the alien devices they'd discovered. "Brian," he interrupted, "could this explain what we found at the crash sites? The level of control over the planes, the precision of the impact?"

Brian added. "That's the fear. These beings possess technology that's centuries, maybe millennia, beyond our understanding. Telepathy, matter manipulation, even glimpses of futures, are all within their capabilities."

Paul and Amy were astonished. The holographic display changed shape, showing detailed schematics of devices that defied conventional physics.

"This technology," Brian continued, manipulating the hologram to zoom in on specific components, "allows for the projection of thoughts and intentions across vast distances. In the wrong hands, it could control vehicles, override security systems, or even influence human minds."

The implications are huge. If terrorist groups like Al-Qaeda had access to such technology, the threat they posed was far greater than anyone had realized.

"But why?" Amy asked. "Why would these aliens share their technology with terrorists?"

Brian hand in air. "We don't know. It could be a dangerous group of them, or they might have an agenda we can't figure out. What's clear is that we're dealing with beings whose motives and capabilities are far beyond what we understand at this point."

Paul dug in his memory, connecting dots he hadn't even realized existed before. "The pyramids," he muttered, almost to himself.

"What?" Amy and Brian asked together, turning to look at him.

Paul was suddenly aware of the theory forming in his mind. "The pyramids, how they have downward columns, the ancient wonders... what if ancient humans did not build them at all? What if aliens have been influencing our development for thousands of years?"

Brian wore a mocking smile. "You're not the first to have that thought. There's evidence suggesting alien involvement in many of humanity's great leaps forward. Even Nikola Tesla's work with energy and frequency—some believe he was in direct contact with these beings."

"Tesla?" Amy interjected, her scientific curiosity piqued. "But he claimed his ideas came from divine inspiration."

"Perhaps," Brian replied, "but what if that 'divine inspiration' was communication with advanced alien intelligence? Tesla's work with energy and frequency aligns remarkably well with some of the technology we've... acquired."

"So, what's our next move?" Amy asked.

Brian's anger got the better of him. "Dig deeper. Find out how this technology ended up in the hands of terrorists, and we stop whatever they're planning next. We can't let people down again."

Paul is no longer lost in his thoughts. "Time to re-evaluate everything about the attacks."

"Agreed," Brian said. "But we need to proceed with extreme caution. If this knowledge became public... it could cause global panic."

Amy suddenly spoke up. "What about the other world powers? You mentioned everyone's trying to get this technology. What do we know about their progress?"

Brian responds. "It's a constant chess game. Russia has made significant advancements, they have a colony in northern Siberia. China is also in the race, although we're less certain about their progress. But here's the concerning part, we've picked up talk suggesting that some Middle Eastern groups, possibly including Al-Qaeda, have been making overtures to these alien factions."

Paul stood tall and stiff. "Could that explain how they managed to pull off such a coordinated attack? Alien tech?"

"It's a possibility we can't ignore," Brian confirmed. "Which is why I'm granting you both top-level clearance to our alien technology division. You'll have access to everything we know, but remember, this knowledge comes with responsibility."

As Brian spoke, he retrieved two small metallic objects from a safe. They looked like advanced smartphones, but Paul suspected they were far more powerful.

"These devices," Brian explained, handing one each to Paul and Amy, "will give you secure access to our alien tech database. They're synced to your biometrics, no one else can use them. Be careful with the information you access. Some of it... well, let's just say it might challenge everything you think and may freak you out, so stay calm."

"Paul accepted the device, surprised by its lightness. As his hand closed around it, a subtle vibration pulsed his hand, as if the object were quietly alerting its hidden power.

"Thank you, Brian," he said. "We won't let you down."

As they prepared to leave, Brian called out one last warning. "Remember, trust no one outside this room with what you've learned here. We don't know how deep this goes."

Paul and Amy said goodbye with a wave. Walking back, lost in thought, Paul realized he'd changed so much he barely knew himself anymore, and wondered if he'd become a stranger to himself soon. Good or bad, not sure?

When they got back to the office, Paul and Amy just sat there, both still processing everything.

Amy spoke. "Paul, this is... it's crazy. What is all of this? Aliens, magical technology, secret colonies... it sounds like science fiction."

Paul responded mechanically, his mind preoccupied and his answer disconnected. " Yes, I am aware."

He trailed off, his eyes falling on the device Brian had given him. He activated it. Immediately, a holographic display sprang to life above the device, showing a menu of classified files.

"Holy," Amy said in slow motion. "The amount of information here... it'll take weeks to go through it all."

Paul agreed already scrolling through the categories. "We need to focus on anything related to the technology we found at the crash sites. If we can understand how it works, maybe we can figure out how the terrorists got their hands on it."

As they got into the files, the hours slipped by unnoticed. They read about reverse-engineered propulsion systems that defied known physics, energy sources that could power entire cities without pollution, and communication devices that operated on principles of quantum entanglement.

But it was a file on cognitive enhancement technology that really caught Paul's attention. "Amy, look at this," he said, enlarging the holographic display. "There's a section here on devices that can enhance telepathic abilities in humans."

Amy scooted in, as she started to read. "It says here that with proper training, users of this technology can influence the thoughts and actions of others from a distance. Paul, do you think..."

"That this might explain how the hijackers took control of the planes?" Paul finished her thought. "It's certainly a possibility we need to consider."

As the first rays of dawn crept in, Paul and Amy realized they had been working through the night. But despite exhaustion, both felt a renewed sense of purpose. They were on the verge of uncovering a truth that went far beyond the tragedy of 9/11, a truth that could change everything people knew and what they knew not.

"We need to put together a report for Brian," Paul said. "But we have to be careful about how we present this info. If it falls into the wrong hands..."

Amy understood the implications. "We'll need to use secure channels only. And Paul... I think we need to consider the possibility that there might be alien influence within our own government. We can't be sure who to trust."

Paul became all business. "You're right. From now on, we trust only each other and Brian. The stakes are too high."

Paul and Amy were so busy with their research, they didn't notice the air shimmering in the corner. A lanky figure was almost invisible unless you knew exactly where to look. Poof! Gone without a trace.

In the days that followed, Paul and Amy threw themselves into their investigation with renewed vigor. They re-examined every piece of evidence from the 9/11 attacks, now viewing them through the lens of alien technology involvement.


October 5th 1:30 p.m. -Washington D.C.

Amy paused the Pentagon attack footage. "Paul, check this," she says, zooming on a frame. "Right before it hits, a weird ripple bends around the plane, like some energy field controlling it."

Paul follows. "You're onto something. Look at this turn," he says, pointing to the screen. "Too smooth, too tight for a manic pilot."

Both stared, speechless, at the impossible thing on the screen.

Paul adjusts his chair, feeling eyes on him. He catches movement from the corner, but turns to empty space, brushing it off as tired nerves.

Paul's phone buzzes as they pack up, a text from Farid, his Afghan contact. He reads it aloud: "They're not alone. The stars have allies on the ground. Be careful." He hands it to Amy, to read for herself.

"Farid's never off. They've got help we didn't see. We've got to turn over every stone and figure this out." Paul said.

Amy grabs her coat, already on the move. "I'll round up the field agents, schedule a call. But Paul, if aliens are tied to these groups, what's that do to global security?"

Paul lifted his hands in a half-shrug. "It's a war we've never fought, Amy. All the possibilities of figuring this out seem to land on us."

They step toward the door, the air behind them warping and changing. Two dark eyes blink into view, staring after them, unreadable, then gone. A high-pitched whine cuts through the room, quick and done, no sign of who left it.

The war on terror twists into a global fight, beyond nations or creeds, stretching across galaxies. Paul and Amy stand at its core, facing a threat beyond their world. They've got to chase the truth down, no matter where it hides.

# Eleven
## *Threads Unraveling*

Tariq Al-Hassan paces the carpet of his motel room, the chill seeping through old windows on Denver's outskirts, far from the dry heat he'd walked into weeks ago. Every footstep outside the door makes him jump, chest pounding, the threat of exposure pushing him to the edge.

He traces the same loop around the room, peeling wallpaper curling like dead skin, the overhead light buzzing. Orders of plan B repeat in his head: hit Denver, take this room, sit tight. Days bleed into weeks, each one making him wonder if they'd forgotten him. Trapped with no way out, the musty stink of cigarettes and the bags of trash tested his limit for today.

The burner phone on the nightstand rings, skipping on the cheap wood. Tariq grabs it so fast he nearly drops it, fumbling, nerves wrecked.

"Are you secure?" a camouflaged voice asks in Farsi, flat and masked.

"Yes," Tariq whispers, scanning the door like a man unhinged. "I've waited forever, what's the holdup?" he breaks, finally spitting out what's been burning inside.

A voice broke in, "Don't worry, the others made it." "Instructions soon. Be ready to move quick." Tariq's call dropped, and he was left staring at his phone, furious. Two months of nothing, then this weak voice—that's all he gets. They left him high and dry, even though he did everything right.

Tariq doesn't know it, but his stay's drawn attention. Three weeks back, NSA data crunchers flagged long motel stays popping up nationwide. Agents dug in, pinning one Denver guest as a possible match to a 9/11 hijacker's known contact.

A covert drone circles high above the motel, dead quiet, its sensors grabbing every ping from below. Miles off, young analysts look at screens in a locked command center, hungry for a break, sifting noise with artificial intelligence, cutting-edge data tools the world hasn't caught up to yet, giving them an edge to chase any connection that moves.


October 7$^{th}$ 2:55 p.m. -Washington D.C.

Eric Chen, a young analyst spots a glitch on his screen in the Pentagon's joint ops wing, where NSA and other agencies bunk together, walls down for the 9/11 hunt. "Sir, you've got to see this," he calls, flagging his supervisor over.

The supervisor shoves his glasses up for the readout. "What's this, Chen?"

"That call to our Denver target, it's not on any cell or satellite grid we know. No origin, nothing. Like it dropped out of nowhere."

The supervisor is excited about a break. "Connect me with Paul Keogh."

Paul Keogh sifts satellite maps in the conference room, hours stacking up as the joint team, NSA, FBI, CIA, chases 9/11's loose ends from their cramped new hub. His phone buzzes. "Keogh," he answers.

"Paul, it's Dave from NSA's signals desk down the hall," he says. "One of my analysts caught something weird in Denver. That suspect list we're tracking. One just got a call we can't pin down."

Paul's drops his file. "Can't pin how?"

"No trace to any network, ground or sky. Our gear's got nothing."

Paul senses a real lead breaking open. "Send it all over. I'll pull Strohm in."

The way Amy Rockwell's hair fell, and her smart outfit caught Paul's eye as she opened the door, revealing an attraction he had previously ignored. He's amazed that she copes so well under so much pressure. "Paul, it seems 'Project Convergence,' those presidential alien files, keeps coming up."

Paul cuts in, eager to spill. "Amy, we just got a hit on a Denver suspect. NSA can't trace the call he took, no source at all."

Amy pauses, then says, "You don't think…"

"I do," Paul says. "Whatever Project Convergence is, it's likely the tech behind that call. I feel it. We've got to move."

Bursting into Strohm's office, they found him with his back to the door, just hanging up a call. His face was bright red – clearly, someone higher up had chewed him out.

"Sir," Paul starts, "we've got a situation."

Brian, unconcerned, swiveled in his chair as they discussed the Denver suspect and the ghost call. "Is this connected to the alien tech we found?" he asks, distracted, unusually so.

Amy steps up. "Sir, Project Convergence looks like a human-alien research deal, kicked off under Eisenhower, buried through the years."

He leaned back, taking it all in, and mirrored her words to buy time. He said flatly, "It's bigger than just terrorists," and pointed away. "Some government groups might've been working with these aliens for years, no one telling the full story." He's feeding them just enough, covering tracks after that call.

"That's what we see, sir." Paul says.

Brian was steaming mad, he couldn't take it anymore and barked orders to get it done. "Here's the play. Keogh, take our best team to Denver, grab this guy. We need what he knows."

"Yes, sir," Paul says.

"Rockwell, get on Project Convergence," Brian added, watching for her reaction. "Who ran it? What they built? How it fits? Bring it all to me first, me alone, before it goes anywhere."

"Understood, sir," Amy says.

They turn to go, Brian calling after them, "Watch yourselves. We don't know who's in this. Report to me, only me. Clear?" He spins his chair away again, back to the wall, like he's itching to jump back on that call.

They both quickly agree, "Yes, sir."

October 7$^{th}$ 7:00 p.m. -Denver, Colorado

Back in Denver, Tariq prowls his motel room, the cryptic call keeping his thoughts hostage. Unanswered questions pile up. The creaking in the hall makes him jumpy, sure that the next sound will be pounding on his door.

He throws on a jacket and hat; he's about to lose it from being cooped up. He just wants some fresh air, away from the moldy and smoky smell, a taste of life outside this run-down place, sneaking out with his head down, feeling the cold night air as he walks over more holes than actual pavement in the motel's parking lot.

Tariq drifts down the dark street, barely lit by sparse streetlights, their weak bulbs fading fast, the drone circling high above snagging his every step, unnoticed. Miles off in the Pentagon's joint ops wing, Eric Chen locks onto the live feed, a rookie's thrill lighting his tone. "Sir, he's moving!"

The supervisor edges closer, eyes on the grainy footage. "Call the locals. I want eyes on him."

Tariq weaves through, hands in his jacket pockets, the call's weird voice circling in his head, camouflaged, flat, wrong, mixing with weeks of silence and the itch of unseen watchers. He'd signed up to strike the west, but now the cause blurs as to what he's tied to.

He rounded a corner and stopped. Two fellas in black suits are watching from a block away, their heads moving weirdly under a streetlight. That weird, perfect swaying freaked him out; he had to get out of there.

Tariq slips into the alley, hugging the brick wall, sweat gathering beneath his cap. Did they notice him? Police? Or something even worse?

His phone went off in his pocket. He digs it out, hoping the battery will last, squinting at a random text: "Get back to your room." He's about to snap; he's had enough surprises. *How did they figure out he was out here?*

October 7$^{th}$ 7:05 p.m. -Washington D.C.

Amy Rockwell crouches behind a metal cart in the Pentagon's archive vault, its wheels creaking under stacks of paper files she's hauled from forgotten shelves. Her laptop propped open beside her pulling the most secretive digital records. Project Convergence hits her like a tidal wave, file after file, yellowed pages and grainy scans, spilling out more than she'd ever imagined, some deliberately left off the system, buried in this lonely corner nobody checks. She flips through Eisenhower's shaky notes on first contacts, JFK's typed memos on alien alloys tested at Wright-Patterson, Nixon's scrawled warnings about telepathic probes in '72, even Clinton's vague logs of biotech trades in the '90s, all before 9/11, all tying aliens into Earth's bones deeper than anyone knows, their tech and minds woven into today's world, their presence walking among us.

She shoves the cart along, its squeak bouncing off the concrete walls, uncovering files for other nations, Russia's crude energy cores from Siberia, China's optic lenses from the Gobi, Britain's sonar rigs off Scotland, each clutching proprietary scraps from scattered alien landings. America's stack towers over them, Amy muttering to herself about keeping the world blind to our advantage, a job that's half the fight. Afghanistan's folder catches her eye, detailing mineral hauls from local mines, rare earths traded to aliens for their colonies' fuel, her fingers pausing as it clicks, Osama's turf, a hotspot for more than just war, a major play unfolding right there.

Her walkie-talkie phone beeps, a chunky Nextel cutting through the vault, volume dialed low, so it doesn't bounce off the walls for others to catch. Paul's crackles in from Denver. "Landed. Target at the motel. Moving in soon. Keep me posted on any Convergence updates." Amy presses the button, a smile she can't help whenever she thinks of him. His check-in feels less like a boss and more like a friend, a warmth she doesn't expect but holds onto.

She presses the talk key again. "Hey, Paul, watch yourself out there. I want you to be safe. This Convergence mess, it's dirty, way dirtier than we thought, files stacked to the ceiling, advanced intelligence running wild, deals with countries and minerals I can't even begin to wrap my head around. I've prided myself on knowing this stuff, and now I'm lost, like a beginner staring at a mountain. Up's down, I don't know who's clean, but you can trust me. I've got your back. Stay aware, okay..."

October 7th 7:20 p.m. -Denver, Colorado

Paul Keogh lands in Denver, ready to tackle whatever waits, his small crew of trusted operatives at his side, each one briefed and primed for the job ahead. He grips the walkie, Amy's warning still fresh in his ears, fueling his focus.

She crackles through the walkie-talkie again, caring and clear. He doesn't let it rattle him, sliding her words to the back of his mind, her warmth hitting him deep, a quiet boost he needs. He turns to his team. "Listen up. This isn't some lone terrorist. We're stepping into the unknown. Be ready for anything."

With respect, his crew sharply replies, "Yes, sir," eager for his leadership in deciphering this alien conversation, once a rumor, now vividly real.

The van rolls into the motel's lot, Amy's last message about global triggers playing in his head. Paul knows change is coming, good or bad he can't tell. He's all in, set on this fight. He tells his team, "This is it. We take him alive, keep him safe and make it back to Washington."

They positioned themselves around the motel like a SWAT unit, trained officers sneaking into place without making a sound, Paul depending on every move they made. Above, a subtle but watchful presence observes their actions, felt more than seen.

Tariq paces his room, certain he's done for, no way out. He breathes in, out, fighting the panic, then a rap bangs the door. Reality slams in, he's not imagining this.

He stops cold, his heart pounding loud, the loudest thing in the room, enough to rattle the thin walls.

"Mr. Hassan? "FBI. Open up."

Tariq stumbles back, arms flailing—window, bathroom, door—searching for an escape, his worst fear is in front of him, no time to pick. The door breaks open, Paul charges in, gun aimed straight at him. "Tariq Al-Hassan, you're under arrest."

They slap handcuffs on him, Tariq quiet, cooperative, a shell, unwashed, dark circles under his eyes, stinking, clothes hanging off, a thin frame who hasn't slept in weeks. Paul spots a light blinking in his pocket. "Check his pockets," he says.

An agent reaches in, pulling out a triangle-shaped metal piece, its gold light dancing wild, nothing human in its make. "Sir, you need to see this," the agent says, handing it over.

Paul holds it in his palm, recognizing the tech from before, but this one is fighting to leap freely, forcing him to grip it and press a button. A nudge slips into his mind, urging "Get out, now," a warning from the hovering presence above breaking through.

Paul trusts it, a message from somewhere he can't place. "Out, now!" he shouts, shoving Tariq toward the lot.

They pull Tariq outside, his legs dragging, when a white flash swallows the room, a shockwave chucking them hard onto the asphalt.

Paul picks himself up, words gone, staring at a perfect hole where the room was, no mess, no burn, just a clean cut in the world.

His team climbs to their feet, the Nextel beeping, Amy breaking through. "Paul, it's starting. Reports hitting from everywhere. Convergence is here."

Paul grabs Tariq by the shoulders, staring into his empty eyes, searching—*does this guy even know what he's holding, what he's in?* He turns back, looks at the void, then around at his men, stunned. These trained forces were frozen by a space wiped clean with no trace. He pictures Amy, his ex-wife Deborah, the American people, the world, even Tariq, all caught in this everywhere war now, alive and rolling, no one knowing what they're up against or what they're defending.

# Twelve

## *Decoding the Convergence*

The atmosphere in Denver crackles with a charge no one can see, the Pinewood Motel's Room 237 now a perfect void, a clean scoop taken out of the world. Paul stood there, dumbfounded, replaying the bright flash in his head. The team around him is focused, meticulously collecting dust, measuring, and double-checking every step.

Agent Sarah Reeves steps up, a blonde in all the ways a good blonde should be, the office's Ice Queen, stunning, untouchable, all business. "Sir, we've swept the area. Nothing's here, no rubble, no heat, no signals we can pick up. That chunk of the building, it's just gone."

Paul, the guy who always follows through, the one you reach out to when the project is too much, single now with office rumors flying about who would win his heart first, too dedicated to work to care. "Tariq?" he called out into the night.

"Secure but shaken." She says. "Medics are with him now, checking vitals. He's fine, far as we can tell."

"Good work, Sarah. Get him ready to move once they clear him. We need him at the secure site for questioning," Paul says, respect mutual between them, she's got a future, and he knows it. "The device?"

Sarah lifts a clear evidence bag, the triangle-shaped metal piece inside dulled, its gold pulse quiet now through the plastic. "It's stopped moving. We've got it boxed off until we can ship it to containment."

"I'm not trusting that with anyone else," Paul says. "I'll handle getting it back myself."

Amy's frantic words were so loud on the walkie-talkie, Sarah and the team picked up bits and pieces. Worse and worse reports came, but Paul just kept listening, storing them away in his head. "Reeves, contact local police and the FBI field office," he instructs.

"Sir?"

Paul leads. "This isn't just us. It's hitting everywhere, all at once."

Sarah dashed off to make calls, leaving Paul staring at the vanished area. It's called Convergence by Amy, and it just completely takes him over, *what's that all about?* Forces he can't name feel real and close, no time to break, just move and fight.

October 7$^{th}$ 7:45 p.m. -Washington D.C.

Thousands of miles from Denver, Amy Rockwell sits at her station reading transcripts of intercepted messages, and feeds from across the globe. She's earning her nickname, the office's human computer, every tap pulling order from mess.

Brian Strohm interrupts her diligence. "Talk to me, Rockwell." The Secretary of Defense stands nearby, suit creased and sagging like he slept in it, hair a mess, a whiff of whiskey trailing him. His usual polish, not so much, a man obviously wrestling his own secrets more than the crisis out there.

Amy acts fast, a perfect opportunity. "Sir, the Convergence protocol means worlds colliding, ours and another realm, no question about it."

Strohm steps closer to hear her out, a naughty tone, the stink of alcohol wafting over as he plants himself near. "Explain."

Amy lays it out, happy to play along. "Project Convergence is a rabbit hole, sir. Aliens have worked their way in, built colonies with us, set off trade wars and treaties across the planet, and it seems like they're the ones running the show. Countries fight for deals with these groups, some over minerals we lack, some for power others can't match. This information, built up for decades, shows without a doubt our world's crashing into another realm. Some aliens want to steer it right, keep the damage low."

He cuts in, gruff and dismissive. "The rest?"

Amy goes on, her words inappropriately giddy. "Osama's crew in Afghanistan, that rogue faction, they've cut a deal. They're letting aliens mine rare earths there, trading it for a chance to turn this shift into chaos, a weapon to grab control."

She grabs a folder from her cart, flops it open on the table, pages spilling out. "It gets worse, sir. The terrorist messages we're catching, they're loaded with talk, not all human. Half's Farsi, half's alien, mixed. They've been teaming up longer than we ever thought, and these files prove it."

Strohm pounds a fist on the table. "You're saying terrorists are speaking alien now?"

Amy pushes more manila folders toward him, stacked with papers from the vault. "A lot of this never hit the system, sir, stayed buried down there on purpose." She keeps her eyes on him as he watches her stack them up. "Human words mixed with something I've never heard, a new language born from both. Break it, and we'll know what they're after."

The room goes quiet, not in a good way, only the muffled voices from the room next door cutting through. Strohm breaks it. "What's our play?"

Amy faces him straight on, pride swelling as she lays out her find. "We crack their code, human and alien both. If we pull that off, we can get out in front of this."

Strohm says, "Do it. You've got what you need. And Amy, be careful who you talk to, keep the hidden stuff between you and me, whatever we talked about today stays in this room, understand? Unless I tell you otherwise." He pauses, then adds, "Get Langley on it, Rockwell. They can help crack this, but only what I clear." She nods, starts dialing, passing the order to the CIA's cryptanalysts. His words, a mix of trust and threat, she feels his approval despite the chill.

October 7th 8:30 p.m. -Langley, Virginia

Beneath Langley's floors, a team of CIA cryptanalysts digs into the code Amy Rockwell's flagged from Denver and beyond. They've been grinding since 9/11, chasing the threads that let the attack slip through, and now they're on this new lead. Seasoned pros bark orders, newbies scramble with printouts, interns haul coffee, all cleared to the hilt, the room a swarm of focus chewing through intercepted messages on live machines.

Dr. Eliza Bern stands at the center, facing a bank of supercomputers going through data, tired from days without rest. They've made ground, no question. Nostradamus-style phrases cracked open chunks of terrorist talk weeks ago. But something is still in the gaps, a part they can't figure yet.

The analyst, Thomas, spins in his chair. "Dr. Bern, I've got something." A kid shoved into this job by his dad's old CIA ties, he's still green, but smart enough to land here.

Eliza steps over, peering at what he's pulled up. A new connection through the terrorist talk, shifting in ways that don't match anything she's seen before.

"Is that..."

Thomas pointed to the readout in agreement. "It lines up with the energy marker from that device in Denver. The aliens' language, it's baked into the terrorists' code."

Eliza straightened through her fatigue. "Tom, this isn't some simple code." she says. "It's a cipher key. They're mixing alien patterns with their words so only those in the know can catch it, and it's not easy to pick up." She turns to the room and says. "Get me a line to the Pentagon. Rockwell's the one to unravel this, we need her team on it now."

The team realizes that no one is leaving until these breaks. Thomas jumps up, stoked, he never thought this gig would land him in alien code territory, grabbing the phone to dial Amy, all of them tied to what's breaking open right in front of them.

October 7th 8:55 p.m. -Denver, Colorado

Paul Keogh stands in Denver's cold weather, watching his team load Tariq Al-Hassan into an armored van, in the motel's lot. The terrorist slumps in the back, hands cuffed, staring off, muttering strings of words that mean no more than air, meaningless to the agents posted at his sides. They're rolling him to a black site, and every second ticks louder in Paul's brain.

A guard steps up, knowing this moment could mark his career under Paul's command. "Sir, you need to hear this."

Paul peaks into the van, close enough to catch Tariq's breath, the ramblings spilling out like a broken faucet. Most is noise, a jumble of sounds, but pieces snap into focus: "The stars align. The eagle falls. New city rises." Paul freezes, the Nostradamus terms hitting, familiar from Langley's briefs. But something else was speaking, a rhythm, words, alive and wrong, like it's reaching for him.

His phone cuts the moment, Amy's message flashing: "Breakthrough in the code. Hybrid human-alien. Call me now." Paul dials, the line clicking as he watches Tariq's lips move, the muttering unbroken. This isn't just crazy talk.

Amy picks up fast. "Paul, thank God. We've got it. The terrorist code builds on Nostradamus, but there's more to it, alien patterns laced in. That's why it stayed buried til now."

Paul keeps his focus on Tariq. "Amy, Tariq's chanting it, the Nostradamus stuff, but there's more, something off, not human. He's our Rosetta Stone, I can feel it."

Amy pauses. "Paul, we need him here, at a site with gear to pick his speech apart, match it to the alien tech markers."

"We'll break this open," Paul finishes, already moving. "I'm sending him your way, full speed."

The team jumps, doors slamming—engines firing—every sound—metal clanging—tires crunching—keeps Paul sharp, worn down but wired, the noise pinning him to the moment. Forces he can't name threaten closer, like walls caving in. Tariq's ramblings rerun in his head.

Across the globe, reports pile up fast. Vanishing spots like Denver's motel multiply, no casualties recorded, as if something's picking its targets carefully. Remote deserts and packed cities alike bend under strange breaks, physics snapping, cracks splitting open, glimpses of a warped, strange world bleeding through.

October 7th 8:55 p.m. -Afghanistan

Farid crouches in a wind-carved nook, his breath puffing white in the brittle chill, every muscle squished as he peers from his hidden perch. The sky above him tears apart, smeared with colors he can't name, blues bleeding into purples, streaks his village elders never spoke of. Something's wrong up there, a shift he feels imminent, not the familiar dust storms or star fields of home. His comms unit, a scuffed box that's kept him alive as a double agent, cold in his palm, its gleam catching the unnatural light.

He presses the button, fingertips raw from cold mornings, his mind cracking under the strain of what he's seen. Words tumble out, but a rush floods his head, voices or static he can't place breaking through him, real or imagined he can't tell. "The convergence, it's happening," he stutters, letting out what's building inside. "The barriers are falling. They're coming through."

Miles off, etched in the mountains, Osama Bin Laden kneels, an oil lamp spitting yellow across the walls, its flame dancing off rough-hewn stone. His fortress stands apart, a warren of tunnels carved deep, a king's den for a man who'd crown himself. Fingers trace prayer beads he's gripped since his fighting days, each knot a tally of his will. Dust from the rock walls cakes his robes, it smells of incense and the unwashed burn of ambition. His followers shuffle through nearby passages, their chants a low roll, but he's alone in this, a madman clutching a vision too big for any god.

A small metal piece, twin to Denver's find, rests in his other hand, its surface crawling with a dull, shifting light. He keeps his eyes shut, visions storming behind them, reality buckling, lands twisting, power bending to his grasp, all guided by a will he claims as his own. He jumped at the chance when those outcast aliens, who betrayed their kind, landed in his reach, promising him rule over the Convergence for the rare earths they rip from his peaks. A smile, slow and unhinged, the look of a man who'd laugh at the world's end. Soon he'll lord over a reshaped earth, or so he believes.

What eludes Osama, beyond the grasp of his alien collaborators, is the force that manipulates them into mere pawns. He's clueless; the Convergence isn't his tool, it's theirs. This new world will reset everything from humans and aliens to Earth and beyond into something nobody could predict.

October 7$^{th}$ 10:45 p.m. -Denver to Washington D.C.

Paul, Amy, and their teams stay connected and push through the night, tearing into the hybrid language. Each breakthrough, each minute of code, a hard-won piece they carry forward against the ticking hours.

Terrorist plots, alien schemes, and evil forces connect faster, gathering into a storm. But in the crack between realities, where uncertainty lies, humans will rise. Minds and spirits together to face what's coming.

Light cuts the sky as Paul stands at the plane's window, eyes on Tariq across the hold, the engines roaring east toward the Pentagon. He peers out, spotting a mirage in the distance, like a rock skipped across a pond. This isn't scaring him anymore, he's past that, a man ready to break anything in his way.

"We're coming for you," a vow Paul throws to whatever waits out there. "Whatever you are, whatever you're planning, we'll stop you."

The plane lands, Paul plants his feet, ready to move. The storm's here, evil converging, but he won't let humanity fade out. They'll fight, they'll overcome, they'll turn this galactic clash into a chance to build something stronger, if they must.

# Thirteen
## *The Informant*

The early winter's coming through Farids threadbare coat. He pulls it tighter, scanning the bare slopes below, his breath a cloud in the dark. This narrow ledge, his new post for a month, offers no comfort against the cold, but it gives him a clear shot at the valley's secrets.

He peers down, picking out a row of large caves in the rock face across the range. Somewhere in that maze, Osama Bin Laden and his crew scheme their next move. Farid's task stays plain: watch, listen, report. Nothing about it ever comes easy.

A gust rips at the rag tarp over his head, threatening to yank it free. Farid snatches it, numb and fighting the old rope back into place. His eyes drop to the metal lunchbox tucked in the corner, its dwindling stash a tally of days against him.

The isolation drives him mad. Farid mutters to the rocks, the wind, anything to fill the silence. He can't risk a radio call, not with Bin Laden's men skittish stalking suspicion. Now he feels alone and helpless.

His hand drifts to his chest, feeling the small lump under his layers. The comms unit Paul gave him stays hidden, his only tie to something beyond this forsaken spot.

As if called by his will, the device goes off. Farid happy to slip it out, went slow, blocking from prying eyes. The message is short: "CONVERGENCE SPEEDING UP. NEED INTEL ON BIN LADEN'S NEXT MOVE. STAY ALERT."

Farid's was upset, chasing what "Convergence" means, a word he's stuttered out himself, one he's caught voices everywhere lately. He's fed Paul intel for months, but these questions hinting at stakes bigger than bombs or borders.

A rustle in the valley below keeps him cautious, alert and clear.

He grabs his binoculars, dialing in. Two figures step from a cave, faces lost in the dark. Farid looks harder, exhaustion dragging at him, a man worn thin by too many nights like this, wondering why he can't just live out his days free of this load. Bin Laden stands clear, his lanky frame unmistakable, beside a stranger with an eerie, water-like move.

Their voices drift up on the wind. "...the veil thins, portals activate, world remade..." Farid shakes his head, catching coded phrases he's tracked for weeks.

The stranger dips his head, precise and deliberate, then turns toward the mountains. Farid catches a glint in the man's eyes, bright enough to pierce the mile between them. For a heart-stopping moment, Farid feels that gaze rake across his hiding place.

He flattens against the rock, thanking himself for picking this spot, tucked behind an outcropping of magnetic ore the locals swear scrambles signals. Whether luck or the stone's trick, Farid senses the alien stare slide past him, uncaught.

As the pair slips back into the cave, Farid lets out a breath he'd trapped inside.

Farid ducks down, reaching for the communication device, hurrying it as fast as he can punch out the message. "Bin Laden meeting with unknown person. Coded phrases repeated. Something's changed. The words, they're different now, more powerful. I think they know I'm here."

As he sends it, Farid knows he's picked a side. The game's changed, and he's no longer sure of the rules or the players.

October 9th 7:45 p.m. -Washington D.C.

Paul Keogh wakes to his phone ringing, cutting into the nap he stole in his Pentagon bunk. Sleep is always last, a gift after too few hours, and he grabs the device, diving straight into the words, knowing a call now spells bad news.

He sits up, seeing coded phrases, a mystery figure, the game changing. It fits their Convergence hunch, and Paul wants to know what comes next.

He pauses over the buttons, knowing a wrong reply could get Farid killed. "Hold your ground. Don't move on them. Get every word you can. Extraction in play. Stay alive." He sends it, hoping his words pull Farid through.

Paul dresses in a rush, shirt untucked, a mess, far from his usual polish, the wear showing through. He strides through the Pentagon halls, looking at faces, wondering who else carries this damned secret.

Amy's already at it in their patched-together strategy room, pale from vending machine junk sinking her health, but hungry for answers, she keeps going. "Paul, you've got to see this," she says, like a champion.

"Show me," he says.

She pulls files stamped with codes he's never seen, markings unfamiliar on the page. "That hybrid language, part human, part something else? I'm onto it."

Paul recalls Tariq's chants stuck in his head, the words he spat out too strange to pin down.

Amy interrupts his thoughts. "Project Convergence changes it all, we're alone in here." She clicks up a photo, Eisenhower, 1954, trading tech with an alien, clear as daylight. The device on the table mirrors the 9/11 wreck's find, no doubt about it.

"You're saying..." Paul starts.

"This tech's ours too," she cuts in, "built over decades. Bin Laden's crew tapped it somehow."

He drops into a chair. "How'd they get it? Why now?"

"Wait," Amy says, going deeper, "here's the link." She flips to a timeline, Philadelphia Experiment, 1943; Roswell, 1947; Cuban Missile Crisis, energy spikes climbing each time. "Project Convergence tracked this from the start. It's been building."

She pulls a sketch, planets crashing together. "Galactic civilizations, maybe other realities, slamming into ours."

"So, Bin Laden's group," Paul says.

"They're playing with controls that could remake everything," Amy finishes, "using tech we helped birth, blind to what it can do."

Paul grips a hoard of papers. "How long?"

"Paul, it's here," Amy says.

The door flies open, Strohm striding in. "We've got trouble. Reports hitting from everywhere, vanishings, reality bending, global now."

Paul and Amy pay attention, Farid's warning burning through them both.

"There's more," Brian adds, "Afghan contacts flagged activity where Bin Laden's holed up. Look."

He pulls up images, Afghan hills warping and folding into portals, a figure stepping through and vanishing.

"What is that?" Paul asks.

Brian points, shrugging it off. "Portals, maybe. Your job to figure it, right?"

The room falls away, Amy tucking the planet sketch onto the big board across the wall, mapping it all. The board stretches past earth now, all of them caught in it.

"We move fast," Paul says. "If Bin Laden's got this tech, we've got to make a move."

Amy back at her station, throws everything she's got at their alien tech data. "I'll spot their next hit."

"Good," Brian says, knocking the desk twice, staring Paul down. "We need eyes everywhere to stop this."

Paul stands, planting his feet hard, a curse slipping out. He's not the one that started this mess, he's the one who'll end it, no matter what.

October 10th 7:30 a.m. -Washington D.C.

Dr. Eliza Bern stands in a lab deep in the Pentagon, a room with thin aluminum walls bolted tight, a few chairs scattered for the assistants or students who filter through. Tariq al-Hassan lies flat on a medical slab, his head a nest of wires and sensors, their clicks breaking the quiet. The space stays bare, just the essentials: a table, some gear, no clutter or junk to fill it.

Eliza turns to her team, pointing at the displays. "You're seeing it, right?" Her heels rise and she smiles.

Dr. Patel, the neurologist lead, peering in. "It's unreal. Those brain patterns don't line up with anything human."

She faces the crew, hands cutting through the air toward the equipment. "This setup pulls from decades of Project Convergence work. It's built to catch thought signals way outside our norm."

Monitors sit electrified with Tariq's brainwaves, green and red lines spiking into wild arcs, mixed with code half-human, half something no one knows. The lab's low throb matches the data's rhythm, pulling the team in tight.

"Roll the playback," Eliza says.

Tariq's words come from the speakers, not his mouth. It's flat and human and with a frequency the machine barely can interpret. "Veil thinning, realities merging, convergence starts, trinity."

Eliza adjusts her jacket, stepping to the display. "Look at this, it's code, it's speech, but together it's a lever for the universe's foundation." She looks around, catching their dazed faces, the hybrid's pull hypnotizing them, unnoticed.

Dr. Patel swings around, caught between wonder and cautiousness. "You think someone planted this in his head?"

"Installed and programmed." Eliza says, "His whole mind's rewired."

Eliza steps back, needing a moment even though she's pressured to get this to Paul's team fast. The Convergence isn't waiting, it's already rolling out.

October 10th 9:30 a.m. -Washington D.C.

A disorganized mess of Farid's intel, Amy's timelines, global reports, and Eliza's lab findings sprawls across the strategy room table before Paul Keogh; he can't unsee it. Theories were tossed around like a ball in a heated debate, every voice pushing to find the answer and claim the credit. Sarah Reeves, the analyst who rises above the rest, new to his team, looks over at him. Her knack for cutting through noise, honed from years unscrambling signals in field offices, sets her apart. No denying it—she's as striking as she is smart, the kind of presence that pulls a second look, and it impresses Paul.

"Reeves," Paul says, "what do you see in these energy spikes?"

Sarah steps forward, her walk confident, like she's done this a thousand times. She starts talking, and Paul feels it hit, a rush slotting straight into his head, clear as a photograph. "The spikes mark vulnerabilities between realities, the decades-old plan before the Convergence kicks in, portals popping open to other worlds." Her voice lands normal, but the ideas stick too fast, too vivid, like she's planting them there.

Paul blinks, thrown by how he's never held knowledge deep as what just landed in his mind. All day, he keeps circling back to her, each talk leaving him with answers he didn't hear her say, details about alien tech, timelines, stakes he shouldn't know yet. By late afternoon, they're in a briefing, maps and photos pinned up, the latest global oddities laid out. Paul's mind is blown by Sarah's Convergence explanation – he's picturing crazy gas clouds, star bridges, and realities melting like wax. They hit like old memories, vivid and real, from a life yet to arrive.

"Sarah, who are you really?" Paul asks after the room clears.

Sarah responds. "You're already piecing it, Paul. I'm here to guide you. The Convergence is in motion, and you've got to see what's on the line."

Paul's mind jumps back to Brian's briefing weeks ago, the Secretary's rundown sticks. Two types they've met, Nordics tall and fair, the brains, Grays short and plenty, the hands. Sarah's face is brilliant in his sight, her too-perfect features and old-soul calm making sense, a Nordic right here masking as one of them. "You've been feeding me this stuff straight into my head?" he asks.

"Had to," Sarah says. "You're the pivot here, Paul. Bin Laden's alien partners, the dissidents, they're pushing the Convergence to claim a world with him as king, but they don't get what they're waking up."

"Why me?" Paul asks.

"You're the one to trust to hold this," Sarah says. "What I've told you, you'll need it for what's coming." She turns away, leaving him thinking.

His phone cuts in, Farid's message: "Something's happening. The mountains became cones and then mountains again. It's crazy here, I can't even describe it. Help me."

While standing there, Paul experiences a deluge of Sarah's downloads—alien grids, reality anchors, and Trinity's form—all flooding into his mind. He pulls himself together, ready to call in the team. He's starting to see the line between this world and another, his next step teetering between here and there, portals cracking it open, keeping it contained. Running this show.

In Denver, he led operations and headed a new liaison team. Now, he serves as the connection between reality here and elsewhere, transformed by weeks of experience, feeling stronger and more self-assured. This war has evolved beyond simple land grabs. Existence itself on the table, Bin Laden and his alien crew with their dirty paws trying to claim it all. Paul's team, the last wall standing for lives across worlds he can't begin to count.

He goes to the window, sees D.C., but his mind's eye shows him different versions of it—some bright futures, some total disaster. Which one sticks depends on him, he feels it settle, he won't fail.

This job has changed him.

# Fourteen

## *Government Secrets*

In New York City, the morning rush stalled. On Wall Street, traders stop shouting, notepads slipping in their hands as they look up. Above the city's concrete ribs, the sky opens, folding in and out. Buildings under construction stretch tall one second, then squat the next, their frames blurring against a sky that won't stay still.

With an apron tied to his cart's handles, a hot dog vendor stands on 5th Avenue. "You seeing this?" You couldn't hear him over all the honking. A block down the street, tourists stared up, cameras swinging. An elderly woman froze, stunned.

Times Square empties out, its giant billboards showing static, skyscrapers too changed to name. Gasps, curses, and prayers replace city sounds. Everything slows down. They just stand there, pinned by something nobody can get a grip on.

Tokyo's office towers turn quiet, workers press their hands to glass. Mount Fuji sits outside, its peak swelling to take over the view, then shrinking to a bump before shooting up again. A salaryman in a gray suit drops his tea, the cup splatting on the floor as he does nothing, too confused to pick it up. Across the city, a grandmother stops sweeping, holding on her broom, watching a mountain that moves like it's on show.

In Paris, tourists clog the Champs-Élysées, necks tilted toward the Eiffel Tower. Its iron frame goes upward, metal beams like they've gone soft. A street artist drops his brush, paint smearing him as he watches, caught by a structure between beauty and wrongness, his art can wait. A kid tugs his dad's sleeve, pointing, but the man just stands there, baguette forgotten in hand.

Moscow's Red Square empties its usual bustle. St. Basil's domes turn into a carnival, their colors changing from one to another. A babushka selling flowers puts her basket down, petals blowing on the cobblestones as she crosses herself. Soldiers near the Kremlin gate shift their rifles, peering up, boots rooted to the stone.

Elders sit cross-legged on the Outback's red dirt. The sun and stars share the sky in an unbelievable daytime spectacle. An old song is hummed by an elder as a dream state awakens around him. This other guy is rocking, like he's heard this ancient tale before.

In rural Kansas, a farmer stops his tractor mid-field, dirt settling around the tires. Trees along the road snap, bending branches, some breaking off fast. He climbs down, sinking into soil that feels off, staring at a sky where clouds have gone sideways. His dog howls, nosing his leg, but he just pats its head, wrecked by the sight, can't move.

No one gets hurt. While buildings sway, they don't collapse; while people watch, they don't fade away. It's quiet, precise, like the world's rewriting itself with care, leaving everyone unharmed, watching something unknown take hold.

October 11<sup>th</sup> 9:00 a.m. -Washington D.C.

Alarms ring through the Pentagon, sending papers flying as staff move between desks piled high with maps and phones that constantly light up. The strategy room was a mess... cracked floor, dirty lights, and clearly hadn't been cleaned in ages. Brian Strohm, in a rumpled jacket, angrily slammed a fist on a stack of reports. He snarled, spitting orders at the aide who fumbled the radio, his grip was slipping with every word.

He barked for a status report, tightening his belt so fiercely it dug into his stomach, his face wincing as his patience wore thin.

Weathered and worn from many sleepless nights, a woman in her mid-30s lifts her eyes from her desk, resembling a machine nearing burnout. Her face shows the toll of this job. "We're seeing strange things happening in all the big cities globally..."

"Get me Keogh and Rockwell. Now," Strohm growls, cutting her off before she's done.

Both battle-ready, Paul and Amy charged through the doorway. Paul's age was apparent in his growing stubble. Amy felt undone, a scientist who almost saw this coming but couldn't yet stop it. "What's the situation?" Paul asks.

Strohm spitting it out rude. "The Convergence is outpacing everything we planned. About time you fix this."

Amy looks at the data, reading the lines, her hope is to find how to fix this. "The steps we missed in the protocol were supposed to hold this back. What shifted?"

"That's your job to figure out," Strohm says, jabbing a button. Cities flash red on a holographic globe. "These are the hot spots. See it?"

Paul pieces it together, staring at the map. "They're hitting populated zones. It's not random, it's a grid, tapping the planet's energy lines."

Amy connects the dots. "Like a network."

"Obviously," Strohm says back, his tone dripping venom. Another alarm blares, and a younger analyst stammers, "Massive spike in Nevada, sir!"

A curse escaped Strohm's lips. "It's on. You two, follow me. You need to see this." He stormed off, so Paul and Amy went after him, navigating strange hallways until they reached an elevator. They end up in a weird, isolated wing. The Pentagon's concrete is gone, replaced with a retro copper and pipe look, complete with gears and cogs from the pre-Eisenhower era.

"What is this place?" Amy asks, checking out the setup.

Strohm reached the metal doors and stopped. "The heart of it all." Sliding open, they reveal a chamber with meshing gears and plates, a spinning central device, and blue light arcing within a metal spiral.

"What are we looking at?" Paul asks.

"The Nexus," Strohm declared, arms crossed. "Our shot at reverse-engineering the Trinity, alien tech we've been chasing since the forties. Decades of failures piled into this, it's got some kick, but it's a counterfeit next to the real thing. Even the aliens who handed it over couldn't crack what Trinity is. It's something beyond all of us."

Amy was amazed as she moved in. The more she learns, the more she realizes the Nexus is in a whole other league – even her skills aren't enough. "How long has this thing been around?"

"Since the fifties," Strohm says, proud like it's a win. "Part of the alien pact."

"Now what?" Paul wants to know.

"Those dissidents are taking over the Convergence." Strohm said, ignoring all our agreements with the council.

The council's briefing at the Lincoln Memorial continued to impact Paul on a deeper level, its significance tied to Trinity, extending far beyond his typical work. "What if their plan works?"

"It rewires everything," Strohm says, "land, minds, us. People out there are already seeing memories that aren't theirs, living in two places at once." Paul's confidence from yesterday gone, doubt tugging at him, but he shoves it down, he's got to hold the line.

Amy steps back from the Nexus. "So, what do we do?"

"We fight back," Strohm commands. "Paul, get to Nevada. That spike is from a site where the outcasts are running. Figure out what they're up to and kill it if you can."

Paul thinks about this, another of Strohm's wild chases wasting time. Something's off about the guy, ticking him off more every second. He can't call it out, not with Strohm outranking him, but it's dragging them down, and he feels it.

"Amy." Strohm says, turning on her, "You're stuck here. Your tech brain's all we've got, make the Nexus work for us." His dismissal hurts, a slap after calling it a failure, leaving her bristling—no respect, just busywork for a dud.

"What about you?" Paul questions digging under Strohm's skin.

Strohm now pissed off. "What's it to you, Keogh? I'm running a global show, keeping the world from falling apart while you play errand boy. Go do your damn job." Poking at Paul, acting like he's still a bad ass.

Paul and Amy leave, Strohm's words chasing them. "One more thing. Keep your mouths shut, Convergence is screwing with heads, and I don't want you two turning stupid. Watch your backs." His sneer digs in, deflecting, nasty as ever.

They get to the common area and into the elevator packed with staffers rushing info between offices. Paul's hand brushes Amy's in the crush, her fingers holding against his, a warm moment they both need in this mess. They're in this together, caring more each day, and it's the only thing keeping them sane.

Quiet settled in as the doors slid shut. They gave each other a moment of support. The elevator stopped, and Paul noticed a strange, moving light. He's writing it off as exhaustion, but it's still on his mind.

They head into the hallway, analysts are everywhere. A junior analyst rushes up, greeting them. "Sir, ma'am, new report."

Paul and Amy listen, ears primed for it. "What is it?" Paul braced.

Pausing, the analyst thought she saw something above. "Nevada's spike, it's blowing up fast. And there's more. Readings inside the Pentagon, like the anomalies outside, but closer. Too close."

"How close?" Paul demands.

She shows us a screen; the building's map is flashing red above. "It's here, and it's moving!" she said. The three of them checked out the ceiling.

The thing hunting them isn't in Nevada, it's here, and Paul's wondering if they're being played.

# Fifteen

## *Alien Tech*

Paul's eyes got used to how dark the Pentagon's underground was. He's tense. Beside him, Amy focused on her device.

"There!" "Elevator!" Amy pointed and yelled. "The reading is strongest here."

Better things occupied Paul than playing hide-and-seek, so he investigated, arms folded. Ghostly apparitions and strange lights fueled his curiosity. Years of training and experience proved useless against this; he felt unexpectedly unsure of himself.

A ping from Amy's device got everyone's attention. "That energy signature," she mumbled, her brow crinkling as she figured it out. "It's... shifting. Almost as if it's stabilizing itself."

A familiar voice cut Paul off before he could reply. From the corner hall, Brian called out, "Stand down... we've got it under control."

Paul's words slipped out. "Sir? What's the situation?"

Defeated by the pressure, Strohm huffed, his posture slumped. "It's time for full disclosure." He says. "Come on, Amy, there's someone you need to meet. Paul, I think you're already acquainted."

As they made their way back to the secure facility they had visited days earlier, they thought through the past weeks of revelation that challenged everything they thought they knew about life.

The room had such advanced technology; it resembled a scene from a sci-fi film. Holographic displays are visible in every direction. Intricate, webbed contraptions reminded Paul of his father's complex fishing net repairs, a distant memory now. What was normal is gone.

At the center of it all stood a figure that made Amy stop in her tracks.

In a softer voice than normal, Strohm introduced Amy to Sarah.

The woman—if she could be called that—turned to face them. She possessed a hauntingly beautiful face, almost too perfect to be real. Her eyes, a crazy beautiful blue and silver, were so expressive, like you could see right into her soul (if she had one).

Sarah's voice, resonant and unearthly, greeted Amy. "I'm pleased to finally have a proper introduction." "Paul, it's good to see you again," she waved to him.

Amy felt emotions wash over her. The scientist in her was awestruck, face-to-face with living proof of the Nordic extraterrestrial theories she'd researched for years. But another part of her, a more primal part, noted the easy familiarity between Sarah and Paul. A twinge of something that felt uncomfortable like jealousy rose in her.

"You're... you're not like us," Amy managed.

Sarah smiled, a gesture both familiar and alien. "Not entirely, no. I'm what you might call a hybrid. Part human, part... something else."

Amy observed Sarah and Paul, noticing Paul's unsurprised expression. For a second, she felt left out, wondering how long Paul had known Sarah's secret.

Strohm cleared his throat. "Sarah has been with us for years, aiding in adapting alien technology. Recent events have sped up our plans."

Paul's wrapping his head around it. "It all points to this technology, doesn't it? That weird energy and everything."

"In a manner of speaking," Sarah said. "What you've been detecting is a byproduct of the technology we've been developing here. Technology derived from my people's knowledge."

Amy's scientific curiosity momentarily overrode her personal feelings. "The 9/11 attacks," she said, pieces falling into place. "Those maneuvers shouldn't have been possible. It wasn't just skill, was it?"

Sadness covered Sarah. "No, it was not."

Sarah stands by the Nexus, laying out a history that upends everything they knew. She points to the wall, tracing paths of ancient alien landings, secret deals with governments, tech that bends what's possible.

"The Roswell crash in '47 flipped it," she says. "We couldn't hide anymore. That's when talks started."

Amy cuts in, piecing it from files they dug up months back. "Eisenhower. Those missing five days in '54, he met your people, didn't he?"

Sarah confirms. "Eisenhower, Kennedy, Nixon, they all knew. The world wasn't ready, so we picked slow integration."

Paul connects it. "The tech jumps, computers, internet, physics, medicine, that wasn't just us, was it?"

"Not all the way," Sarah says. "We've nudged you along, aiming for the galactic fold. Too fast, and it breaks everything."

Strohm flips on a display, a map shows up across the room. "We've teamed with her people, tweaking their tech. MIT, Johns Hopkins, Caltech's Jet Lab, they're all in, splitting the work."

The map lights up, dots all over the States. "Jefferson Labs in Virginia builds energy weapons," Strohm says, gruff as ever. "Penn State handles propulsion. Texas runs quantum computing."

Paul takes it in, the scale taking hold. Sarah steps up. "The dissidents don't like slow. They're pushing to remake every world their way."

"Where does Bin Laden fit in?" Amy asks, curious.

Sarah answers, "He's their pawn, blind to it. The dissidents saw his drive as a chance to use him for their ends. The cost is all of us."

Paul digs back to old intel, Bin Laden's early days. "His family's ties, the money, the schemes, it wasn't just oil and buildings, was it?"

Sarah shakes her head. "The Bin Ladens knew about us for generations. Osama chased those secrets, ditched the wealth for it."

Amy puts it together. "The dissidents gave him the answers."

"And tech to cross into madness," Sarah says. "The 9/11 devices were the start."

Paul brings up the Trinity units, the metal triangles from the Pentagon wreck he's tracked since day one. "Trinity units. Each hijacker had one, right? That's how they flew so clean, steered by the golden rod."

Sarah answers, "They link the mind to the plane's systems, overwriting controls. Flight 93 failed because the passengers fought back, breaking the hijackers' focus, crashing it before it hit the White House."

Silence settles, hitting hard over Flight 93's heroes. Paul mulls Bin Laden, a guy like that with power this big.

"What about the grounded planes?" Amy asks.

Strohm cuts in abruptly, controlling the talk. "We've tracked some tied to follow-up hits. They're off the map now, still packing alien gear, we think."

Paul asks, "Anything from our man out there?"

Strohm shrugs it off with a chuckle. "Nothing solid, Paul. The last word, he'd dig deeper for the truth. Maybe he's in Bin Laden's crew, maybe not."

Concern for Farid is unspoken—if he's caught, it's over for him and the mission. Paul asks, "Next move?"

Sarah steps in, hand up like she's got it covered. "We'll match them. This tech's just the opener. Our gear tops what the dissidents gave Bin Laden. Trinity works better for us, in hands that know its secrets."

She waves at the wall, a panel sliding back to show devices that defy sense. Glasses, a watch, a cube small as a die, others too alien to name. "Mindlinks, reality anchors, gravity shifters." she says, picking up the cube. "This is a reality anchor. It pauses the Convergence, keeps you in your own reality."

Amy eyes it all, itching to grab it, a kid in a candy store barely holding back. "The Convergence, you said it could break it all. How?"

Sarah lays it out, "The dissidents want realities merged, them in power, their way. Those global anomalies are their first stabs at control, but they can't wield it right, not like us, with the Council's know-how and Trinity's communion with us."

Paul gets it. "Bin Laden thinks he'll rule it, a god-king."

"They sold him that," Sarah says. "The truth's messier, riskier."

Strohm cuts in. "There's more. We've got a group in our own ranks, big shots on black projects, motives unclear, no oversight."

Paul asks, "What's their play?"

Strohm spits out. "They want control after the Convergence, maintaining power their way."

Amy says, "And they don't care who pays."

Sarah says, "They're about to screw it up, wrecking all worlds."

Paul sees this fight on multiple fronts, Bin Laden's crew, this cabal, the Convergence itself. "So, what's the plan?"

Strohm points to the red dots. "These are the hot zones, Convergence grid markers."

Sarah says, "Build a network to block our enemies, tap the energy grid to find their devices, shut them off."

Paul starts plotting. "I'll get teams at every location."

Strohm joins in. "I'm pulling Special Forces, CIA, scientists, anyone cleared for this."

Paul's sees Farid's code flashing. He steps aside, speaking quietly. "Farid, you, okay?"

"Paul," Farid says, "time's short. I've seen stuff you wouldn't believe. Bin Laden's not running it, the aliens are. They've got plans, bigger than he knows."

"What plans?" Paul asks.

"Not safe here," Farid says. "A takeover. He thinks he's king, they laugh at him. It's their game, Paul, we're nothing to them, none of us."

The line drops. Paul turns back to the group. "Farid. He's alive, but maybe in trouble."


October 11<sup>th</sup> 3:50 p.m. -Afghanistan

Hidden in a cave, Osama Bin Laden holds a high-tech device, as if it were his birthright, a king's treasure. In the middle of the room is a large table piled high with meat and bread, he tears into it, getting grease all over his fingers. On either side sit aliens, their skeletal forms motionless, ignoring the feast, food means nothing to them. He remains unconcerned, the golden rod's stolen energy on the table, always within his view.

"Soon," Bin Laden says, "we'll shape the world for Allah. I'll be his vessel, steering humanity into a new age." The aliens sit quietly, a pack humoring their pawn, cloaks pulled tight over their forms, laughing under hoods to mock him. He misses it, lost in his own glory.

One alien, the leader, fixes its barely-there eyes, black slits, on him. It speaks without a word, the thought sliding into Bin Laden's head. "Yes," it says, barely hiding its amusement, "a new order, sure." Bin Laden agrees, smug, blind to the jab.

The device glows, power swelling. Bin Laden keeps eating, not touching the tech until he's done and cleaned up, his eyes never leaving it. The Convergence nears its peak, existence on the brink, the golden rod feeding the chaos he thinks he'll rule.

October 11$^{th}$ 5:50 p.m. -Washington D.C.

Paul Keogh and Amy Rockwell sit at the strategy table, scribbling reports to send Brian, pens scratching over maps and notes. They grabbed for the papers at the same time, and Paul brushed against Amy. She looked up, met his eyes, and he said everything would be alright.

Paul shares his feelings. "Never thought I'd miss chasing terrorists. This mess is eating me up, Amy. Everyone out there... our families, our people, they're vulnerable, clueless about what's coming. How do we save them? I'm scrambling here, and it's tearing at me."

He pauses, then adds, "Brian's off lately too, pushing us around like he's covering something."

Amy gave a small smile, warm with care. "It's a lot, Paul. But we're in this together, all of us. We'll figure it out."

They turn back to their reports, finishing the stack for Brian.

The dissidents play Bin Laden like a fool, laughing at his pathetic grabs while they take the minerals they need, striking gold with such an idiot. A cabal in their own government ranks, chasing power through the cracks, Brian reeking of corruption too messy to trust. Paul and Amy stand between them and everyone else, fighting to hold the line for a world slipping fast.

# Sixteen

## *The Cover-Up*

The cold cuts at Farid as he peers down from the hillside with his binoculars. The season digs deeper, thinning his stash. He rummages through a beat-up sack, fishing out a bruised apple for a quick boost, counting days on what's left. He ate and got back up to get to where he was going.

Farid serves as Bin Laden's trusted lieutenant, or so they buy. He catches wind of hushed meets with al-Qaida grunts spilling crazy talk, aliens, gadgets, the world turning inside out. Weeks of mirages, portals, and those freaky dissidents slap him awake, nothing, what he thought he knew. He signed up to stick it to the bad guys with Paul, not dodge mind-reading space jerks who might sniff him out any second. Now he's stuck, questions piling up with no end.

As he gets to the village, two figures glide from a crevice, swishing side to side like they're floating, not walking. Bin Laden's alien crew. Paul pegged them as dissidents in that last call, off-worlders, outcasts. Farid ducks behind a boulder, fed up with these weirdos, craving the life he'll never get back.

He gripped the device Paul slipped him, a hidden comfort against his leg. He hopes Bin Laden's goons miss it. Something big brews, and he's got to tip Paul off, even if it's half-baked bits he can't piece together.

He is there. Stone rolls back from the opening, a cavern too huge to make sense. Farid blinks, rubbing his face, but it stays real, no mirage this time.

"Farid, the Sheikh wants you," an al-Qaida thug barks, poking his head from the gap.

Farid went deep inside, reaching a cavern with crystals hanging down and a floor like glass. He wakes as energy hits him. This isn't his usual watch post. Having only seen it from a distance before, the up-close view makes him nervous.

A wide expanse unfolds, its pathways branching into numerous work areas, held together not by walls but by an invisible, magical demarcation that Farid perceives as remarkable. This is all new to him, and he's captivated, discovering secrets around every corner.

"That's quite something, isn't it?" A cool, friendly thought enters his mind. Farid saw a dissident looking at him. "This is New Eden, Farid. The new world starts here." "Bin Laden's paradise, his chance to rule the world."

Farid holds like a poker player. Emotions could blow his cover, and he's not letting them peek inside.

"The Sheikh's waiting," he says out loud.

The dissident sweeps an arm out, mocking a grand invite. Down in the city, Farid sees humans and aliens busy with machines he's never seen before. Up ahead, a wall screen flashes a turning globe, red lights across it.

A gold tower, morphing as they watched, held figures in its windows, defying gravity. A metal and crystal device at the base powers it, the top spikes appear to be its controls. Bin Laden stands there puffed up, as if he owns the place.

"Ah, Farid," Bin Laden says, turning with a big, toothy grin, mocking him under the words. "Come see our new age kick off."

Farid steps up, and the dissident butts in. "Preparations are almost done. The Convergence hits its peak soon, reality's walls ready to disappear."

Bin Laden is pleased. "I stand atop reshaping the worlds for Allah."

Farid spots the alien's mouth twitch, a quick, creepy smirk. "Sure," it says. "But your old pals are stirring trouble fast."

Bin Laden questions. "The Americans? What do they know?"

The dissident waves a hand, a display popping up with Paul, Amy, and intel faces Farid knows. "They've linked with the Council. They're handing your kind the Trinity and the power that runs it, could mess up the plan." Farid is trapped, knowing he's deep now that his crew's on screen.

Farid stands there, this "council" meaning nothing to him. He's lost on who they are and feels betrayed by every side.

Bin Laden touches his beard. "What's your move?"

The dissident's eyes stare. "A show. Something to slap humanity down, prove they're nothing.

The creature spills the plan, and Farid's hands sweat, heart pounding. He's got to warn Paul, but he's cornered, Bin Laden's guys and these aliens all boxing him in. He's played it safe for years, risking it all for the good side, and now he's kicking himself for it, stuck in this mess with no clear out.

A scuffle kicks up at the entrance. Two dissidents drag in a supply runner that Farid knows, struggling between them.

"We caught this one sniffing the perimeter," one says, its thought full of scorn. "His head won't bend like the rest."

Bin Laden spits on the ground, looking over. "A spy?"

The dissident shrugs, picking up some human swagger. "Maybe. Or just nosy. Either way, he's seen plenty." This one's hung with Bin Laden's crew too long, copying their moves, likely laughing at them when they're not looking.

Bin Laden turns on Farid. "Handle it, friend. Prove we've got this to our allies."

Farid's ticked, stuck in this spot. He knows the drill, kill the guy, prove he's in. But the villager's face begs him, and Farid can't swing it, even with the world on the line.

He decides fast, sliding to his weapon, plotting escape. Pain brands behind his eyes, knocking him off his feet, like they've burned his plan out of his skull.

The lead dissident stands, hand out, teeth bared, licking its lips. "You let me down, Farid," its words boom. "I expected better."

Darkness takes him, and Farid's last hope hangs on Paul catching the warning he almost sent.

October 12<sup>th</sup> 2:40 p.m. -Washington D.C.

Paul Keogh lounged on a worn-out chair, staring at the equipment across the room. He's been roughing it here for days, tired but wired, using a makeshift setup just to grab some sleep between shifts. Determination keeps him going. He waits for Farid's signal to show up. The last call left things unresolved. *Is he okay? Did he make it? What went wrong?*

Amy Rockwell sits in a chair she pulled close, catching the sausage biscuit Paul tossed her. "Still nothing?" she asks.

"Nope, nothing," Paul says, wiping egg off his shirt. "Something's off with Farid. During the last call, he sounded like he had more to say and couldn't. Days since he checked in, and it's killing me. I've got a feeling he's in trouble."

Strohm knocks on the door, a rare courtesy knowing Paul's been holed up working non-stop. In the middle of a bite, Paul yells, "Come in." Brian marches in, trailed by two figures whose wide, flawless faces are clearly extraterrestrial. Paul's coffee splashed, sandwich falling. He shoots up, wipes crumbs, acting nonchalant despite the huge mess and important visitors.

"Paul, Amy," Brian says, looking tense and holding something in. "Zar'vok and Lyra are here to rescue us!"

Zar'vok stands tall, crisp in his stance, a pro who's seen decades of this game. "Your tales call us Nordics. Our truth runs deeper than that."

Lyra glides forward, her words slipping into their heads, high-pitched like helium, pure. Zar'vok's assistant is her title, her job is delivering crucial intel related to Council maneuvers. "We've tracked the dissidents. This isn't good."

Paul gets serious. "What do you got?"

Something's bothering Zar'vok. "The rebels are making their move on the Convergence."

Amy chucks her wrapper. "What are we up against?"

Lyra flicks her hand, an image pops up, a device of crystal and metal, nodes of energy connecting inside. "This is a Mindlink," she says. "It connects to the brain at the root and controls it."

Paul asks, unsure. "So, the dissidents have one of these?"

Zar'vok says. "They'll tie it to the Convergence, when reality's walls vanish." Brian cuts in, ego loud enough to cringe. "What's their advantage? What does it do?"

Lyra shares. "They like to control minds at the root."

"The brain chip," Amy says. "How's that tied to the Trinity?"

Zar'vok confirms. "It rewires brains, changes memories, wipes free will clean. They want a new race, no free will, slaves to their rule. The Council's Trinity keeps that choice alive, and that's the fight."

Paul says. "And Bin Laden's role? How's he fit?"

Lyra jumps in. "A puppet. They fooled him with global control talk, his perfect Allah-state. It's a sham. They'd never hand a human that power."

Brian snaps, impatient. "Their real play?"

Zar'vok lays it out. "Total rule. They aim to craft a world they've plotted for over a decade. Earth as the first domino. Win here, and they'll sweep every plane."

After a minute of quiet, Paul says. "How do we shut them down?"

Lyra says. "We've built our own tech, weaker right now but a start. It'll be ready post-Convergence to counter their Mindlink technology."

Amy grabs her sketch pad, doodling fast, a nervous tick more than notes. "How will these match their Mindlinks?"

"How do we stop these links from working? Are they using it now? How many have they implanted? What's their plan? Everybody?" Paul also asks.

Lyra pulls her collar down, pressing a button on her suit, smooth and quick. "The Mindlink needs massive power, not easily available. That's why they're with Bin Laden's crew."

Paul presses for more. "What are they getting from Bin Laden?"

"A rare mineral in those mountains," Lyra says. "Processed right, it boosts the Mindlink. Bin Laden's outfit digs and refines it for them."

Zar'vok adds. "They've got too little to max it out yet. That's kept their moves small."

The room absorbed Paul's ominous words. "They are capable of eliminating us on any given day."

Brian barks. "We move now. I'll pull anyone cleared for this. Do it. I said DO IT!"

He spins to Zar'vok and Lyra, ordering again. "Get your people, whatever you've got. We need it all."

Lyra and Zar'vok stay cool, seeing through his deceit but letting him yap, free will their game.

The group draws out plans, but Paul can't stop thinking of Farid. The doubts strangle him inside, no word if his friend's alive or dead, no contacts to check, no failsafe he'd set up, and it's tearing him apart.

October 12$^{th}$ 2:55 p.m. -Afghanistan

Farid wakes to pain, searing his skull. His head pounds, thoughts dragging slow, like wading through mud. His vision clears, revealing a featureless room. Its walls are white and pearlescent, cold from within.

He heard a voice in his mind: "You're awake." Farid shrinks back. The dissident stood before him, his flawless features betraying only clinical curiosity. "Your mind holds up well. Most humans break under our interrogation tricks by now."

Farid tries to speak, but his mouth stays shut, refusing his will. The alien's mental voice shifts, laced with amusement. "Don't bother talking. We've paralyzed most of you for now. Can't risk you pulling anything stupid, can we?"

The alien keeps talking, and memories surge back. Farid recalls the hidden base, odd devices, plans for a crushing power display. His heart thumps fast as he grasps the threat to his allies.

"I admire your loyalty to your American friends," the alien says, circling Farid as he lies on the floor. "Misguided, but still impressive."

Farid wants to spit defiance at the thing, but he manages only a hard look.

The alien sighs, mimicking humans too well. "No point hiding it now. You've seen too much, know too much. But maybe you can still serve us."

It reaches out, pressing a long-fingered hand to Farid's forehead. The touch feels like death, sending fear through him. "Your mind carries secrets, key operatives, communication details. With our tech, you'll give it all up. Better yet, you'll make the perfect trojan horse."

Farid is angry now that he knows what they're up to. They're trying to use him as a weapon against the people he's supposed to protect.

"Don't worry," the alien offers, its mental voice dripping false comfort. "You won't feel a thing. When it's done, you'll march loyal in our new world order. Nice, right?"

The alien starts the process, but alarms break out. Its head jerks up, and neck stretches 2 feet. "Impossible," it mutters. "They can't have tracked us this fast."

Farid acts fast, putting all his will into it. He struggles against paralysis, forcing first his fingers, then his whole hand. Too busy with the outside ruckus, the alien misses it.

The creature turns around, and Farid grabs it by the throat. The thing stumbles back, pulling him along. They hit the control panel, and Farid suddenly wasn't paralyzed anymore.

Desperation makes Farid move like a rocket. He quickly grabs a weapon-shaped piece of alien tech and rams it into the creature's head. With a determined focus, he willed the thing to fire.

A searing flash erupts, leaving the alien crumpled and lifeless, its eyes staring blankly. Immobile for what felt like days, Farid stood, his body stiff and aching.

Alarms blare on, combat sounds bouncing through the base. Whatever's happening gives him a slim chance to escape and warn his allies.

Farid snatched the alien gun and headed into the wild mess outside. He's navigating through the corridors of the base, but the real battle is waiting up ahead.

Battle noises ring around him, human yells, alien shrieks. He clutches the stolen weapon tight, praying it works if he needs it.

He rounds a corner and runs into Bin Laden's men, panic splitting their ranks. "The Americans!" one shouts. "They've found us!"

Farid's stops. Americans, here? It feels unreal, but he welcomes the luck. He pulls on his lieutenant act and gives orders. "Regroup at the main chamber! Protect the Sheikh at all costs!"

The men follow orders, rushing toward the base's core. Farid heads the other way, aiming for what he hopes is an exit. He needs to reach the Americans, warn them of the dissidents' scheme.

A familiar voice halts him at a junction in the cave. "Well, well. What do we have here?"

Farid slowly turns, facing Khalid Sheikh Mohammed, Bin Laden's Ops chief. The man's eyes, suspicious. "Fleeing the fight, Farid? Not your style."

"I was looking for you," Farid lies. "The Sheikh needs every man, and we have got to guard the tower."

Khalid stares long, face unreadable. Then he lunges, a curved knife flashing in his hand. "You always were a bad liar, Farid."

Farid dodges, the blade cutting air where his throat sat a second ago. He swings the alien weapon up, but Khalid kicks it from his grip.

They grapple, each scrapping with the fury of a last stand. Farid lands a solid punch, knocking Khalid back. He steps in to finish it, but dizziness hits, a leftover from the alien's mind jab.

Khalid pounces, slamming Farid to the ground. The knife dives down, and Farid grabs his wrist, stopping it inches from his face. They strained, locked, neither giving in.

An explosion rocks the base, deafening. Lights blink out, plunging the corridor into black. Farid knees Khalid's groin in the fight, blasting the air from him. He scrambles up, grabs the weapon, and bolts blind down the hall.

Emergency lights all on, casting a freakish red glow. Khalid's heavy breathing trails him, still chasing him despite the hit. Farid rounds a bend and hits it all head-on.

The hidden chamber burns as a battlefield. American special forces clash with al-Qaeda fighters while dissidents unleash wild power, twisting the place into strange shapes.

Osama Bin Laden stands in the thick of it, face blazing with rage and panic. "Start the device!" he roars. "Take this reality now, before it's too late!"

A dissident randomly hits controls in the main control center. The core of the vortex intensifies, becoming stronger.

Farid acts fast. He lifts the alien weapon, aiming not at Bin Laden or the dissident, but at the control tower. He sucks in a breath, pouring all his might into the shot, picturing it unleashing hell.

Dead center on the control tower, his impact triggers a powerful blast of bright light. It all went still for a moment. Then, BAM! A screech like a trapped animal, and the thing explodes in a flash of light.

The shockwave knocked Farid off his feet and into a wall. He caught a last look at the room before losing consciousness. With their plans blown, the dissidents scattered. Bin Laden's face showed only shock and anger.

Darkness claims him, and Farid knows no more.


October 13<sup>th</sup> 3:40 p.m. -Washington D.C.

This report differed from Keogh's usual paperwork. Updates could explain the near-global catastrophe. Field teams provided live updates from the destroyed base. Paul scans for anything missing, any sign of Farid, clues to what came next.

"So, is it over?" he asked, breaking the void.

Amy Rockwell, exhausted but driven, read report after report. Strohm stayed nearby. The alien allies observed silently. Nordics and Shifters remained calm under pressure, unlike humans.

"It's never over," Strohm emotionless. "The headquarters is destroyed. We pulled valuable alien technology and intelligence. We crushed alien operations and crippled al-Qaeda's leadership."

Amy wants data. "What about Bin Laden?"

"Vanished," Paul stated. He gripped the report tighter. "Along with high-ranking al-Qaeda operatives and an unknown number of dissidents. We bought time. Nothing more."

Zar'vok came forward. He warned them, "That's all they need—time." "The dissidents aren't defeated. They're going to regroup. Cities are still vulnerable to their remaining firepower, which they will deploy.

A sigh escapes Lyra's lips. "That's why we're here. Your species stands at a turning point, and you can't face it alone." She placed a hand on Paul's shoulder, giving both reassurance and care. "We want to help you fix the balance. To train your people. To equip you for what's coming."

Paul appreciated her words. It was a call to arms, disguised as comfort. With good cause.

Holographic schematics and weapon designs filled the room.

"Neural interfaces," Lyra began. "A direct link between mind and machine. Energy weapons capable of phasing through solid matter. Shields that block reality manipulation before it can even begin. Advanced propulsion systems that could revolutionize human space travel. Medical breakthroughs that could eliminate disease and extend life spans."

Amy studied the projections. "This could help in medicine, science, even space exploration."

Lyra continued, "And it already has. We've worked with your people before. Some chose the right path. Others corrupted it."

Paul knew exactly what she meant. Black projects. Hidden labs. High-ranking officials had their hands on this kind of tech decades ago, yet they buried it, hoarded it, and weaponized it. They had played god while the rest of the world struggled for crumbs.

Lyra looked over. "Some of your most powerful leaders were trained for this. They saw the future, then turned against it. Some of them now stand with the dissidents."

Paul was quietly fuming. Governments, intelligence agencies, and foreign powers all struggled for control, with this war's origins deeply embedded within their structures. Regular people had no idea what was unfolding behind their backs.

Amy adjusted her seat. "Then we don't just need weapons. We need to know the people we can trust."

Paul looked at Lyra's display. "How could something this major have been hidden for so long? "

He turned to Strohm. "Any word on Farid?"

Strohm didn't react. He remained still, aloof, offering no help or expression. The lack of concern made Paul mad.

"Nothing confirmed," Strohm finally replies, dismissive and bored. "He was spotted fighting Bin Laden's forces during the raid, but when the base collapsed, we lost him. Search teams are combing the area."

The words stung Paul. He stared at Brian, trying to read him, but the man remained detached like Farid had been a minor inconvenience, nothing more.

Paul subdued his anger. Farid proved to be a valuable resource. A friend. A confidant. Abandoning him felt like betrayal.

"We'll find him," Paul said, more to himself than anyone else. "Whatever it takes."

The conversation shifted back to logistics, strategy, battle-readiness. But Paul's thoughts kept circling back to Farid, to the bad guys regrouping, to the technology that had been hidden from humanity for decades.

The dissidents were still out there. Bin Laden was still breathing. Farid was either fighting for his life or worse.

It wasn't over. Not by a long shot.

October 13th 4:05 p.m. -Undisclosed Location

A tall shape moved artfully in the darkness. The dark hid it, but jerky movements marked it as non-human. It had this bizarre, mesmerizing charm.

Its unseen audience received a telepathic message: "Human performance has exceeded expectations." "Their ability to dismantle our renegade elements was impressive."

Another voice, this one dubious, chimed in. A short-term interruption.

"It's possible," the first one acknowledged. "But underestimating them would be a mistake. They have proven themselves capable opponents. And now, with the Council's technology in their hands..."

A human coldly interjected, "It makes no difference," with finality. "The Convergence is in motion. Life and existence itself will change. When the moment arrives, no level of advancement will protect them from what is coming."

The first one stayed quiet, lost in contemplation. A hand went up, producing a holographic projection. Battered and unconscious, a man was in a containment pod. The casing's nameplate displayed the name Farid Azimi.

"Very well," it finally said. "We continue as planned. But remember this, on the chessboard, the pawn that reaches the other side becomes the most powerful piece. We would be wise to consider that as we position our own pieces."

The display went out, and the room was dark once more. They would be ready.

October 13th 4:37 p.m. -Afghanistan

The damp, cold place smelled of earth and something alien. Farid Azimi's consciousness returned gradually. He was hurting all over.

Shapes shifted around him. A figure sat cross-legged, its face obscured by a weird, wavy wall of air. It didn't speak; it just put thoughts directly into Farid's head.

"You have made quite an impact, human," it said, amusement laced with fake respect. "We did not expect Osama's headquarters to be destroyed."

Farid tried to respond, but his mouth dry and rough. The alien gestured, and a cup of water materialized beside him.

"Drink," it commanded. "We have much to discuss."

Farid took the water and drank, struggling to piece together what had happened and how he got here. The last thing he remembers was inside the dissident base, the explosion of the chamber. Now, he sits in an unfamiliar space, face-to-face with a being unlike any he had encountered before.

"You wonder who I am," the being says. "I represent forces that have taken an interest in you, Farid. We recognize your potential."

Farid forced his voice to work, though it came out hoarse. "Potential for what?"

The alien was surprised Farid could talk for himself—now it was really interested. Galaxy-deep eyes watched him. "For altering the course of history."

As Farid's strength returned, he began to wriggle. "This is not a game."

In his mind, he heard the alien laugh. "This game has spanned galaxies and dimensions, existing long before your species."

Alien intrusion raised Farid's tension. "The rebels, the Council...they're just pawns, right?"

The alien gave a shaky nod of agreement. "Now you begin to understand. But let me show you something. It may help you grasp the full scale of what is at play."

It lifted a hand, and a portal formed in the air. Through it, Farid saw impossible landscapes, worlds beyond limits, civilizations that defied any knowledge he may have. Lights of energy wove through each reality, linking them in ways his mind struggled to process.

"This is the multiverse," the alien explained. "An infinite existence, all connected. Convergence, the force your people fear. We are only at the beginning."

Farid stared, unable to look away. The images shifted, showing great wars across galaxies, ancient powers rising and falling, entire realities bending and reshaping. "Why show me this?" he asked.

The alien's approach felt increasingly unsettling. "Because you have a choice to make. One that will determine the fate of not just your world, but countless others. The humans you fight alongside see only the surface. They do not understand the true stakes."

Farid's settled down, enough for him to focus on what this being was saying. "And you can?"

The alien confirmed, "Yes, we do." "We have guided events for eons. In this war, the dissidents and the Council are insignificant. They're clueless."

Farid's instincts screamed to run, but he stayed put. "What do you want from me?"

The alien rose, its form changing as it moved. "We need you to be our agent. Our helper among humans. You will help us steer these last events toward a favorable outcome."

Farid exhaled slowly. "And if I refuse?"

The alien stood a statue, unmoved. "Then you will return to your people. But without the knowledge I have given you. Without understanding the real stakes. You will move blindly, just another pawn on the board. You be nothing. You will be like them."

Farid closed his eyes, finding himself. He thought of Paul, and how much they trusted each other. He'd vowed to protect this mission, this world. Trapped in the multiverse, he needs to survive.

He said, "I'll do it," firmly. "But I have one condition. No half-truths. No manipulation. If I am to be your agent, I need to know everything."

The alien studied him before agreeing. "Very well. But knowing the truth is not for the weak. Once you learn it, there is no turning back."

"I understand," Farid said. "Tell me everything."

Something creepy started happening in his mind, and the walls around them seemed to vanish. Farid listened, unable to change his mind.

# Seventeen

## *First Contact*

A sleek Gulfstream C-37A descends rapidly onto an Arizona airstrip, its engines roaring as Convergence anomalies cause static interference in the controls. Dessert bursts under the tires, dust rising as the plane comes to a stop. Paul lets out his breath, relaxing his grip on his seat. Amy looked relieved, the same as him. They landed safely, despite the uncertainty. Sarah's sitting alone, stone-still, opposite them. More than just beautiful, the Nordic woman possesses a captivating essence that Amy admires, unaware of her own subtle charm.

Sarah stands. "We're here. Welcome to my home."

A warm October breeze blew in as the cabin door opened. A lone scorpion, the only sign of life, skittered silently across the cracked earth in the quiet, sun-baked landscape. Raw and simple, the air carries the scent of sage.

Paul shielded his eyes from the sun. "I see nothing out here."

Sarah answers. "Look again."

A floating device appeared out of nowhere, flashing. With Sarah's press, air rushes out, causing waves that ripple like those from a thrown stone.

Suddenly, a dome appears, its translucent, curved shell glowing like a second sun. The world's bleak endgame faded for a moment as Paul and Amy stood in awe, a glorious panorama filling them with wonder and breathtaking beauty. Sarah stays unfazed, routine in her step.

"Welcome to New Harmony," Sarah says, opening a seamless slit in the dome as she walks through.

A wave washes over Amy and Paul as they enter. Inside, paradise found. The colony is so captivating that they pause every two feet to take it in. Alive and growing, vines of pretty green weave through the stretching crystal spires that reach for the top. Rivers carve paths through the earth, their waters shimmering with prismatic light. Everywhere you look, there's a flow of beings—some with long limbs or shifting bodies, others so human they'd be impossible to distinguish from anyone else. Tech and nature blend.

Amy says, "Unreal."

Sarah allows pride to hold. "Decades hidden from your world, one of many sanctuaries we've forged on earth, safe havens to live and prep for what's ahead."

The colony's depths are revealed step by step. Beside small, gray-skinned workers and their illuminated gadgets, tall and graceful Nordics glide by. Always moving, the shifters adapt to every moment, flowing like liquid metal. Every being is in sync, unified by a single harmony.

Reading their minds, Sarah gives them answers. "The Grays, our allies for centuries, craft wonders. The Shifters wield quantum tricks, able to support any need."

Curious, Paul bent down, picked up a little crystal, and felt how heavy it was. How do you all keep aligned?

Sarah answers. "Good question. Come see."

She leads them to a pod of living crystal. Two chairs sit inside, devices like helmets floating above, tethered by who-knows-what.

"Thought Bridges," Sarah says. "They link non-telepaths to our network."

Amy steps forward, eagerness trumping apprehension. Paul follows, trusting her lead.

Sarah got the devices in place over their heads. "Relax. Open up. It'll hit hard at first, but it's safe. I promise."

The devices settle, and the room drops away. Amy and Paul experience a surge of thoughts and feelings, their minds interconnected in a vast network. Lots of voices, but they sound like one.

Sarah's guides. "This is our life. Connected, unique, sharing everything."

Brian and Amy are all in. The Grays concentrate their efforts on the machines, the Shifters develop dynamic ideas, and the Nordics provide steady, purposeful direction. A shared ambition creates a cohesive and tightly bound colony.

"Let me show our history with your people." Sarah says.

The scene flips. They stand in a hangar, February 20, 1954, Edwards Air Force Base. Eisenhower stands firm, suit pressed, covered with wartime grit, gray hair thinning under the lights as officers flank him. A silver craft slices down from the night, landing perfectly. Zar'vok steps out, tall and

Nordic, hand extended. "President Eisenhower, I'm Zar'vok. We've got a lot to cover."

Time blurs. Zar'vok unloads cosmic threats, reality's merger, humanity's guardian role, showing tech sketches and devices that leave Eisenhower's mind wild. They finish at dawn two days later, Eisenhower striding out, softened by awe, rushed by necessity, yelling to his aide. "We need an agency for this. Move."

July 22, 1969, Camp David. Nixon lurks in his study, flask tucked in his jacket, paranoia jerking his frame. A phone rings, his aide warning of a visitor. A wood wall slides back from a hidden panel, and Zar'vok appears. "Mr. President, urgent business."

Nixon rasps, "The moon landing..."

Zar'vok cuts in, dry. "A small step." He pauses, Nixon's flat stare killing the jest, then shifts serious. "Signs show reality cracking already. The timing we gave Eisenhower for the Convergence speeds up by decades. We need to stay in control."

Nixon sitting in his leather-tufted chair, stunned, pulling the flask out to pour a glass, hands shaky from too much drink, hiding it from Zar'vok as the words sink into his shrewd mind.

Visions zip past, 1897, Aurora, Texas: a cigar craft smashes a windmill, its alien pilot buried under a cross. 1942, Los Angeles: guns blaze at a hovering shape, shells bouncing off. 1947, Roswell: debris sparks endless whispers. 1966, Point Pleasant: Mothman sightings sync with sky lights and static. 1976, Tehran: jets chase a glowing orb, gauges frying mid-flight. Sarah brushes their hands, a deliberate human gesture she's learned, steadying them through the rush.

The sights vanish. Amy and Paul are back in the present. Sarah pulls the helmets off. "See what we've kept secret for years? The precarious balance we've maintained."

Paul stands up. "The dissidents want those minerals for their Mindlinks, don't they? To strip everyone's free will. You're against that."

Sarah agrees. "Yes, they crave the energy to fuel it, to control the Convergence's fallout. We guard choice, they'd kill it."

Focused on the minerals, Amy cuts in. "Those minerals from Afghanistan, how do they work? We could stop this if we cut them off."

Sarah answers her as she leads them out. "They channel interdimensional energy, focusing it like a lens."

Frustrated, Paul removes his tie, the villains are too far ahead. "That technology is already in the wrong hands."

Sarah joins the exchange. "And they'd rip it all apart, ruling whatever's left when realities merge."

As they walk, Sarah points ahead. In crystal groves, little alien beings with long or shifting limbs scamper about, their laughter echoing through vine-covered walls, creating a scene of vibrant, fairytale-like joy as alien families gather.

Amy marvels. "You've built a utopia here."

Amy's praise, so rare for the reserved scientist, makes Sarah beam with joy. "We've tried. The Dissidents keep us on our toes, blocking pure peace."

They reach a wide-open space, beings congregating under a canopy of light, a center with Trinity symbols, looking like a place of worship. "The Heart," Sarah says. "Where we gather, connect, plan what's next."

Walking up are two Nordics, a Gray, a Shifter. Sarah greets them.

One Nordic speaks, mind warm. "We've waited for you. Time's short, we've got important work to do."

Paul squares up, soldier mode on. "We're in. But why us, why now? This has run decades without us."

The Gray, "We're ready to go. Teams are trained, we've got squads set."

Amy says, "Then let's start. Tell us everything." Usually quiet, she's done waiting, her old life of lab solitude feels small now, and she's ready to fix this or end it.

The Council briefs them, words piling fast. Amy and Paul soak it in, the colony's peace a fragile shield against everything outside.

They stand teachable, adaptable, trusting this Council's calm certainty, yet doubts linger, human instinct kicking up.

Sarah rests a hand on Amy's shoulder while she looks at Paul, assured. "It's a lot. We've watched you for millennia, waiting for this. The threat's here, we'll get through together. We believe it."

A Gray approaches and expresses his thoughts: "Your openness and determination are invaluable. I have witnessed years of this struggle, and your willingness to join us is a source of continued motivation."

It adds, "The Convergence defies the sacred. We've guarded the truth forever. A force. A balance under all existence."

Amy asks. "What force?"

The Gray weighs its words. "Many names across stars. To you, God, or the Trinity, light, matter, spirit. The root of all. It needs guarding, for the enemy seeks to steal free will with the Mindlink."

This hits home, pulling Paul back to his Catholic kid days—altar candles, hymns, a faith he'd drifted from but meant a lot to him, still does. Amy holds still, piecing it.

Sarah interjects. "More later. For now, strength and faith carry us. Trinity binds past, present, and future. We keep it alive together."

A Shifter ripples, its words landing like a good memory, soothing as an old letter. "We're alike, seeking truth, bonds, purpose, the Great Divine. Together, we'll forge something brighter."

Sunset paints amber through the dome's shield, hiding New Harmony from the world. Amy and Paul stand at history's fork, decades of secrets cracking open to humanity's multiverse role.

New Harmony gives them all hope, humans, aliens alike. This unity breeds strength. It's worth the fight.

# Eighteen
## *Worlds Beyond*

Paul sat on a bench outside the Pentagon, attempting normalcy with a cup of coffee. The world was a mess—all chaos and noise, falling apart. Yesterday's peace in New Harmony occupied his mind. Farid's silence was killing him inside. Each day felt like a year, and he felt worse for doing nothing. Though they hadn't known each other for long, they'd become like brothers working together. Shivering, Paul couldn't sit still. He headed for the office. He drew strength from the stillness.

Inside, Amy met him in the hall, waiting near the door as he walked in. She'd been watching him from inside. "Still nothing from Farid?"

Paul got teary, a rough huff escaping him. "Not a word. It's eating me alive."

Before she could answer, an officer stepped into the hallway. "Strohm wants you both. His office and right away."

They moved together, winding through the halls to the Secretary's door. He didn't look up as they stepped inside, just said, "We've got a problem." No hello, no preamble, just that, blunt and cold.

Paul waited, feet planted. Amy stayed beside him, quiet. Strohm began speaking. "The Statue of Liberty's melting into the harbor. Pyramids in Cairo are lifting off the ground. London's sky turned a sick purple. Everything's going bad, and it's everywhere." His voice carried bitterness, like he was daring them to argue.

Paul took it in. "Nothing is considered sacred now."

"It's here," Amy said.

Strohm went nuts; the noise echoed. "Wake up, you two. The aliens warned us. Sure, we torched Bin Laden's headquarters," he said, laughing through it, "bought ourselves a little time, but this thing," he laughed again, "this Convergence, it's speeding up. You think you're both hotshots who can stop it? We're running out of clock."

Paul asks. "Sir, how do we stop it?"

Strohm kept losing his mind, like it was all a joke they didn't get. "Our best are scrambling, Keogh, and they're coming up empty. Not that you'd know what 'best' looks like." The insult is harsh, dripping with contempt.

Paul's pocket was going off. He grabbed his phone, shouting "Yes!" when he saw it was Farid. "It's him!" he yelled, overflowing with happiness and extremely loud. "He's alive! Oh my God, my friend's alive!"

The message was short: "Bigger than we thought. New players. Meet in Northern Virginia. Trust no one. -F"

Turning to Amy and Brian, Paul spoke rapidly. "He is in America, nearby!"

Amy grabbed his sleeve. "Where exactly?"

"NOVA." Paul declared while making his way to the door. "Our designated secure location." A lottery winner couldn't have grinned wider than he did out of gratitude.

A hard, sudden grip from Strohm revealed a look of dark resentment or disgust. Paul's happiness seemed to burn him. A flat, forced "Be careful," escaped his lips. He couldn't stand to see others at ease; his own suffering poured forth like a toxin.

Amy yelled at Paul to be careful as he ran down the hall. She was scared for him, and something else she couldn't put her finger on.

With a skidding stop, Paul turned and gave her a fast, intense hug. Looking her in the eyes, he implied his meaning. He departed, leaving it unsaid.

October 15th 1:16 p.m. -Northern Virginia

The safehouse sat off a quiet gravel road, hidden by acres of government land. A person stepped out of the building. Farid, but different. His eyes carried a strange depth, like he'd spent too long staring into places humans weren't meant to go. Trauma, maybe, or whatever he'd seen out there.

Paul clapped his shoulder, half-hugging him like a brother. "Farid, is that you in there?" He laughed, but the question was real.

Farid's smile came in worn. "It's me. Just beat up. I've seen too much, it changed me." His voice didn't sound quite like Farid that Paul remembered, but it was him, buried in something sad.

Paul squeezed his arm again. "Your message said new players. What's up? Who are they? And man, I'm just glad you're okay, buddy." He pulled Farid into another hug, making it clear this wasn't small for him.

Farid checked out the security guards nearby. His body tense. "Not out here. Inside."

Paul waved off the guards. "Give us a couple minutes."

They slipped into the building, the door locking with a click behind them. Farid didn't waste time. "The aliens we fought. They're pawns. There are powers above them, running a war across realities. And they want you involved, Paul."

Paul blinked, baffled. "Who? What powers are you talking about? Me?"

Farid's stare was unflinching. "They're beyond us. That's all I can say."

Before Paul could push, the room dissolved. Time and space fell away.


October 15$^{th}$ 1:18 p.m. - Beyond Time and Space

Alive and crisp, a clear wind vortex roared around them, a storm you could see through. It rushed past, clarifying Paul's senses. A light beam stood at the center, entering his mind.

In his mind, he heard the word "Paul." "We've been expecting you."

Paul's hand shot to his gun, only to be stopped by Farid. "Hold on, man. They're not here to fight."

The living light shifted, seeding ideas in Paul's consciousness. "I am an Architect. We shape realities, test worlds. Earth is ours to observe, and you help hold its future."

"All this—the nightmare, the deaths—is this your test?" Paul raged. "The world is collapsing, people are in pain, and you're just watching?"

The Architect reassured. "Struggle refines you. We offer a choice, not a command. Free will matters to us."

Farid stepped in. "They're giving us a shot, Paul. A chance to make this right."

The light intensified, deepening to a rich purple. "Decide. Expose the truth and unite your people, or let division destroy them. Choose."

Paul paused, reconsidering his anger, Farid's survival overwhelmed his rage with gratitude. "I've been trying," he said, yelling at the entity, "I tell what I can, what I'm allowed! I've got bosses, rules, I'm not the one calling shots!"

The architect said firm, yet fatherly. "Discern better. Your authorities may not see everything."

Farid said, "He's right. We can't trust everyone above us," and winked at Paul.

Paul clammed up. Farid was here but changed. The world felt stolen, and he was lost. Then he stated, "We tell the whole world. Enough to pull us together, not enough to break them. They need to know. Fear can't win."

The Architect had guided him there, but the choice was his own, born from his free will.

The Architect's light softened, like that was the answer it wanted. "So be it. Act quickly. The Convergence is here."

The vision collapsed, dropping them back into the safehouse.

October 15$^{th}$ 1:52 p.m. -Northern Virginia

Back in the warehouse, Farid stepped outside. "Got something to show you." He returned hauling a couple of metal boxes from his Jeep, stashed nearby in secure storage, prepped long before this mess exploded. He set them on the table, unpacking a sleek recording device—super advanced, 100% alien-made.

Paul dialed Strohm, who answered rudely. "You got something for me, Keogh?"

"We're doing this," Paul said, unflinching. "The hold-up's over."

Strohm stuck back, "What, you're the big boss now?"

Paul, a professional through and through. "We have no choice. We're going public, aliens, the Convergence. It needs to get out, or there's no tomorrow. Get ready."

Strohm huffed, loud and obnoxious. "Oh, really? Fine, I'll set it up. Hope we don't all die," he cracked, as he hung up.

Farid flipped on the device. "This broadcasts a hologram worldwide. Every corner, everywhere. No one's left out."

Paul eyed it, impressed. "That's a hologram machine? Where'd you get it?"

Farid said, "Don't worry about it. Long story. It's ours now."

They moved fast, time slipping away.

October 15$^{th}$ 2:04 p.m. -Washington D.C.

Strohm stormed around the War Room, a caged beast unraveling. His control was gone, ripped out from under him by Paul's move, and it showed. He turned on them, all nasty and mean. "This is it, people! Aliens are real, the Convergence is hitting us, and there's no turning back! We're breaking the silence today!"

Furious, the General leaped to his feet, face red. "You've known how long?"

Strohm whirled on him, sneering. "Long enough! What's it matter to you? We take charge now, or we're done, I don't care what you think!" His words flew like acid, his grip slipping further.

Orders barked out, forces scrambled, intel locked tight. The truth was breaking free.

October 15<sup>th</sup> 6:04 p.m. -Washington D.C.

A global alert sounded, a sharp beep piercing the night's silence. From everywhere, people looked up. Paul, powerful and resolute, appeared as a colossal hologram in the sky, a beacon-like figure stretching to the horizon.

Breathing in, he recognized this as his opportunity to lead and instill hope. He announced, "People of Earth, we're not alone!"

Presented as evidence were clips of UFOs, declassified documents, and hints at the Trinity and converging realities. The world held its breath, listening.

October 15<sup>th</sup> 6:10 p.m. -Washington D.C.

The President stood on the White House lawn, staring up at Paul's face in the sky. His security detail hovered, but he barely noticed. He felt useless, a leader outmatched by something more important than what he knows. Advisors urged, "We need your response now."

He nodded, eyes still on the hologram and speaks "We knew this was possible. Set up the press room. It's time."

A pivotal moment in history was marked by global shifts, with him at the helm.

# Nineteen

## *Crossroads*

The world shuddered as the Convergence tore through its seams. At Stonehenge, ancient stones shook with a rhythmic loop, and the air thrummed with the voices of thousands. Prayers clashed in a dozen languages, some rose in desperate hope, while others cracked with dread. Men and women dropped to their knees, babbling in ecstatic trances, as a preacher screamed of demons clawing free from the earth's core. Above, the sky fractured with streaks of gold slashing across it, as if a beast were breaking out to pull down the heavens.

No corner escaped the mayhem. In Varanasi, the Ganges turned blood-red, boats capsized as pilgrims wailed and plunged into the water, seeking salvation or an end. At Uluru, the massive rock groaned as if waking; its surface rippled, while elders chanted against a wind that howled with beings not their own. Clocks stuttered worldwide, minutes stretched into hours or collapsed into seconds. Birds fell from the sky in droves, their wings useless against the unseen current. People everywhere stared up, torn between rapture and terror, whispering judgment or invasion, unable to decide if this was doom.

Teams of specialists raced against the Convergence of evil, hauling reality anchors to the zones hit hardest by the Convergence's early tremors.

These machines, forged from human grit and alien secrets, were working, anchoring reality where it frayed most, in cities where buildings changed into impossible form and villages where the ground swallowed itself whole. They fought to hold the world together, to shield the millions caught by this, buying time before the fabric of existence split wide open and left humanity stranded in nothing.

October 18th 8:08 p.m. -Afghanistan

The desert cold bit into Paul Keogh harder than he expected as he stood in the doorway of the crumbling Afghan airbase, staring at the stars. No warmth lingered there. Less than a day after Stonehenge, urgency had yanked them here, chasing the final node. The upheaval back home had splintered the chain of command, and trust crumbled. Paul was wrecked, even the top ranks in D.C. felt off.

Exhausted, Amy and Farid sat inside, slumped in chairs with their feet on the table. The Convergence's rapid advance overwhelmed them, and the airbase's frigid air chilled them to the bone. Despite the equipment, Amy's quiet voice carried. "Time's running out, Paul." Every tick slipped away like blood from a wound. She looked drained and wondered if anyone even knew she was missing.

Paul looked around. "He said, 'I know.'" Seeing her like that broke his heart; he was falling for her. He aimed to be a hero but was utterly defeated.

Amy's murmured, "I feel like we're finished."

Paul shushed her. "Don't go there. We're not giving up yet." It was just a challenging moment.

World events had forced them out of Washington, and there he'd caught whiffs of rot in their own ranks. Brian Strohm's name hadn't crossed his lips yet, but the man's ties to the Convergence and alien tech bugged him. Too many red flags.

He kept his suspicions to himself, away from Amy and Farid. Doubt chewed at his insides. If Strohm played a part, the government might be using the Convergence as a weapon for their own ends.

Farid looked up from his chair. "It's worse than we thought, Paul. The rogues have rigged this for months. Hours remain before they light the fuse."

Paul responds. "We're in this, Farid. But let's be real, we're up against the impossible."

Farid's half present, "I saw it. They've been at this for months. We don't have a chance."

Paul slumped down, feeling crushed.

Farid looked his way. "I didn't see it all until now. These aliens aren't here to back terrorists, they're using them. They crave power, and earth's their playground."

Paul thought hard. The dissidents hungered for domination, not just upheaval, and the government's murky role made it all curious. Brian's moves didn't add up; they were too slick, too quiet. Something stank.

Amy smacked the screen a few times, coaxing it to life. Hot spots flared where the Convergence was strongest. "We strike now, or it's over. That node activates, and the Convergence rips us apart."

Paul's readies. "I'm with you on that. Round up the team, we're rolling now."

October 18<sup>th</sup> 8:41 p.m. -Afghanistan

Helicopter engines roared through the hangar as Paul, Amy, and Farid grabbed their gear. The plan was simple: hunt the rogues to the node, smash their tech, stop the merge.

Farid's instincts were razor-sharp from months on the run. "No one's watching us, right?"

Paul checked his rifle and let out a growl. "Can't swear to it. We're as hidden as we get."

The airbase squatted alone in the desert, but Paul stayed wary. The chopper would dump them at the mountain's edge. They'd trek the rest on foot.

As Paul boarded, Amy asked. "Are we compromised? Something's wrong. Strohm's sitting this out too easy."

When she said that, Paul just froze. Brian's absence reeked of deceit. Paul knew. "Trust no one until, we're sure." Later, they'd root out the traitor in their own house.

Amy knew Paul agreed, but they had a mission to finish.

October 18<sup>th</sup> 8:50 p.m. -Afghanistan

En route to the final node the copter ride choked on the tension. Farid stared at the sky; Paul ran through 9/11, alien plots, secret deals, and this world-shattering merge. It buried him.

Paul elbowed Farid and asked, "New players? Who?"

Farid kept his eyes ahead. "There's a lot of break-off groups. Some arm terrorists, others chase entities I can't name. They're all in deep."

"Strohm know this?" Paul spat, the question broke free.

Farid's answered. "Maybe. Maybe too much."

Paul couldn't face that truth yet.


October 18<sup>th</sup> 8:53 p.m. -Afghanistan

Exhausted and dropped into the freezing black, the climb was a Herculean struggle—hesitation meant death.

Paul took point, and Amy swept for signals. Somewhere in those peaks, the dissidents primed the node to shred reality. Paul kept on, mission-locked, but questions stayed with him. Could Brian be trusted? If not, how far did this run?

# Twenty

## *Technological Edge*

Paul felt the mountain wind cut at his face like a knife as he traversed the pass. Frozen gravel held his boots, climbing was a real fight with each step. He heard Amy stumble and gasp behind him, she'd tripped on a rock. Farid moved forward, his mind on his people's safety, something he couldn't guarantee. The cold overwhelmed Paul. Fear gripped him. This was uncharted, overwhelming. Good people didn't deserve this.

"Farid, you're sure we're close?" Amy's asked.

"Satellite pinned it. Energy's spiking. They're about to trigger it. We've got no time," Farid said, urgently.

Exhausted, Paul acted for Amy and Farid. He was emotionally hollow. He'd stared death in the face before, but this was a whole different level. He loathed the dissidents who wanted to destroy everything. He longed for comfort but found none. He briefly pictured his ex-wife. Not now. Just focus on the mission. They pushed on.

October 18th 9:22 p.m. -Afghanistan

Paul dropped flat at the ridge's end, waving Amy and Farid down beside him. Below, the faction's facility sprawled across the valley. They could see down into it: a mash-up of alien and human design, hybrid beings skulking like scavengers, feeding off each other in a cannibalistic frenzy. Guards patrolled the perimeter, some human, others not, their weapons attached like an arm.

Amy pointed to a huge structure. "That's the node. We hit that."

Paul says. "We go quiet. One slip, and we're meat." The defenses were merciless, alien figures moved with levitation alongside human grunts, all armed to kill.

Farid gestured to the side. "Side entrance, less guarded. We can sneak in."

Amy held onto her scanner. "Inside, I'll need time to shut the node down."

He looked at her, as if seeing her for the final time. "We'll buy it. Move."

Under the night, they slid down, blending with the rocks. Noise filled the facility's corridors.

Paul gave the floor a little tap, his pistol was a comforting weight.

Amy took the lead, scanner in alert mode. "Control room's close."

Paul felt his blood pressure surge, without a way to calm down. Farid's eyes, once half-shut with exhaustion, were now wide open—this was too serious to let fatigue win. One mistake, and the Convergence would wipe them from existence.

They reached a heavy door. Paul shoved it open with a grunt.

October 18<sup>th</sup> 9:42 p.m. -Afghanistan

The control room looked deceptively simple at first... sterile, clean, like an empty janitor's closet, but it felt wrong, too vacant, as if it ran itself. A massive, pulsing metal and light tower, like something alive, dominated the center.

Amy raced to a console and plugged in her device. "I'm in!" she said. "But this is a nightmare, alien logic tangled with human code. Someone from our side built this."

Paul bit the inside of his cheek until it bled. A traitor. Strohm? Maybe. "How long?"

"Too long." Amy muttered, hands racing across the controls. "It's fighting me."

The node went haywire, the room shook, lights flickered, and the air vibrated.

"They're starting it," Farid shouted from the doorway.

Paul focused on the node's light. "Amy, now!"

"I'm trying!" she snapped.

The door flew open. Guards stormed in, weapons blazing.

Paul shot instantly, taking down two enemies before they could respond. Farid picked up the fallen rifle and opened fire on the swarm. The walls were riddled with bullets, energy blasts everywhere, a total bloodbath. They were trapped and outnumbered.

"Amy!" Paul shouts, taking down another guard.

"Almost there!" Amy's voice nearly drowned by the node's shriek.

A loud bang filled the air. Blinding light flooded from the node. Ears ringing, Paul stumbled. Amy's shout was unheard by the room, then, the world dissolved.

October 18$^{th}$ 10:14 p.m. -Beyond Time and Space

Paul's head pounded, visions swimming as he dragged himself up, body scraping against the white floor. The air unnatural, like breathing through a mask. His body felt disconnected, far away.

"Amy? Farid?" Paul cried out.

Nothing.

Panic overtook him. The node had detonated, but this wasn't death. A rift? A trap? The Convergence was meant to merge worlds, not strand him in this place. *Or was this it?*

Someone emerges slowly, deliberately.

Paul watched as the shape came into focus.

Brian Strohm.

# Twenty-One
## *Web of Deceit*

Paul's knees let go, dropping him to the floor as the node's collapse caught up with his nerves. He was blinded by a bright light, or so he thought. His lungs felt like they were on fire, a chemical taste burning with each gasp. The world went crazy, a vast, cold white nothingness, and the ground was shaky beneath him. Endless nothing, no start, no finish.

There he was—Brian Strohm, right in front of him. The man who'd led them through fire, who'd earned Paul's trust, now making him question what reality was.

"Paul," Brian said.

Paul pulled himself backwards into the wall, leaning on it to stand, dizziness owning his head. "Where are we?"

Brian looked off. "We had a solid plan. Everything was going to be good for everybody."

Paul spit blood as he spoke. "You've been lying to me. To all of us."

Brian turned to him. "I didn't want it to end this way. You, Amy and Farid, you were perfect for this. When it's finally done, you'll understand why it should happen."

"Understand...really?" Paul was pissed and bitter. "People are dead, Brian. Missing. Whole lives torn apart, not because of the Convergence, but because of what you and your rogue bastards did with it. That's on you."

Brian smug. "You're still blind, Paul. But you won't be for long. We're not giving up just yet. You may think we've failed, but this isn't over."

The void shuddered, folding in on itself. Then Paul stood in the Afghan mountains, the cold again biting his skin, the rocky earth solid underfoot. Brian no longer with him.

October 18$^{th}$ 10:16 p.m. -Afghanistan

The facility lay in ruins, smoke filled from the node's wreckage. Amy groaned nearby, pulling herself up, while Farid moved to his feet, looking filthy, like he'd worked a coal mine.

"Paul!" Amy called out. He rushed to her, helping her as she put a hand to her head.

"What happened?" she asked.

Farid scanned the debris. "The node's gone. Collapsed. It felt like the world split open."

Paul confirms out loud. "It's Brian. I saw him in another space. He's not just involved, he's running this. The Convergence stopped, but he's still playing us."

Amy asked, "Brian? You are certain?"

"He admitted it," Paul said. "He's been using us all along. Whatever he's after, he's willing to sacrifice everything for it."

Farid rolled up his sleeves. "That makes sense. The government shadow group, the aliens, he's their linchpin."

"We'll find him," Amy said. "He doesn't get to walk away from this."

Paul couldn't stop thinking about what Brian said. The Convergence had halted, yet the cost lingered. Lives lost to the rogue faction's greed, not its purpose.

October 19th 2:23 a.m. -Afghanistan

The bunker's walls were a safe welcome. Paul sat there, wondering if he'd ever have a normal life again. He pictured his comfy apartment, his escape from always having to be "on". Silly to think about now but he needed that. Amy was across the room, completely engrossed in some old map. Farid zoned out, leaning against the wall.

"He is disgusting," Amy said.

Paul engages with her. "It's not just him. The Convergence was never meant to kill. It was supposed to connect us, worlds, people. But Osama, the cabal, those aliens turned it into a weapon, an evil one. Now there's blood on the ground. That's what keeps me up."

Amy looked at him. "You couldn't have known."

"Maybe not," Paul said. "But I should've seen Brian's hand in it sooner."

Paul went up to the outside roof, the Afghan sky full of stars once again. Amy joined him, settling close. "You did what you could," she said.

He stared out. "I keep seeing them, the ones we couldn't save. It wasn't supposed to end like this."

"No," she agreed. "But we stopped it. And we'll stop Brian too. Together."

Farid met up with them. "There's something I've been hiding." He hesitated "An implant in my head. The shadow group put it there when I was captured. Not the aliens, the human group tied to Brian. It's how they've tracked me."

Amy was surprised. "Farid, why didn't you tell us?"

"I didn't know who to trust," he admitted. "I thought I could outrun it, remove it. But if they activate it, I'm done. Or worse, I'm theirs."

Paul chucked a rock off the roof. "We'll get it out. You're one of us."

Farid was relieved.

October 19$^{th}$ 9:12 a.m. -Arizona Dessert

In Arizona, Sarah stood before the Council, a mix of human leaders and alien delegates from across the globe, united under a fragile truce. Her hybrid heritage made her a bridge, her expertise made her a great leader.

"The Convergence is over," she said, addressing the room. "The dissident's version, motivated by greed and power, collapsed with the node. But its original purpose wasn't destruction. It was connection. We lost people because of what they did, not because of what it was. Now we build something better together."

A human delegate chimed in, waving their hand. "You're saying it could happen again?"

Sarah's calming presence filled the room as she spoke. "Not like that. We'll shape it, a framework to unite worlds safely. Starting here, our home, then beyond. A galactic council, if we're bold enough."

Conversations took over the room, agreement taking root. Sarah glanced at the empty chairs reserved for Paul, Amy, and Farid. Their fight and courage paved this path.

# Twenty-Two
## *Unlikely Allies*

The Pentagon's Artificial Intelligence Center was tucked away in the building's secret depths. In 2001, it was Amy's quiet haven, a no-nonsense space where she'd poured years into data science and AI. This project was hers, started way before everything went sideways. The room was basic. Computers crunched data, screens showed numbers and patterns, all made to figure out what was coming next. Some of it, alien tech from places like Jefferson Labs, but it wasn't showy. It just worked better.

Junior staff moved around, testing algorithms and tweaking robotic arms sorting objects. A lead analyst approached Amy with printouts. "We kept things running while you were out there saving the world," he said, looking at her with quiet pride. Amy smiled at him, then turned to an intern. "We're using real-time data now. It spots anomalies fast and predicts issues ahead."

Paul walked in confidently, feeling good after some much needed rest and clean clothes. He stopped beside Amy, close enough to stir something in her. "This feels important," he said.

She looked at him. "It is. This is my work, Paul, knowing what's ahead." As she said those words, she thought of how good Paul smelled, a mix of soap and something uniquely him.

"What about the Mindlink?" he asked.

"It's meant to connect us," she said. "Brian manipulated it. I still think it's important. It can be done right."

"If we keep it in safe hands," Paul said.

"That's the plan," Amy assured.


October 30$^{th}$ 10:00 a.m. -Washington D.C.

The briefing room was all about connecting the dots. Amy stood at the front, the microphone ready, next to General Davis. A screen showed the AI center's feed. Davis spoke first. "We're building tools to stop threats early."

He gave Amy the floor. "The AI's handling incidents already before they become a problem. Predictive models let us move fast. The Mindlink could connect leaders worldwide fast. It's about teamwork, not power. It's a way to look ahead, to keep people safe so this doesn't happen again."

A media person raised their hand. "What if someone like Secretary Strohm gets it?"

"This is something I've been a part of since the beginning," Amy explained. "It's not just mine. I've had help from the labs, from alien tech. But it's my baby and I'm in charge. It's meant to help, and we'll make sure it stays in the right hands. It's for good, not harm."

Davis stepped back to the microphone. "We've cleaned house with the Council's help. Now we're setting up something lasting with our partners globally."

He continued. "That's where this is heading. Cooperation will be essential. The Council we've started forming, along with key international partners, will ensure a peaceful, long-term solution."

The media person heard that before.

October 30th 1:46 p.m. -Washington D.C.

Amy stood before her team, teaching them about alien energy patterns. She'd been given the authority to lead this now, her team growing under her. She was in charge, a quiet victory after everything with Brian. Paul sat in the back, supporting her, raising his hand like a student. "So, it's not just ours anymore," he said.

She smiled. "It's for everyone. The Mindlink could tie it together, real-time across borders, for telepaths and regular people alike. It helps communication without barriers."

Paul yelled out without raising his hand. "Brian wanted control. You're sure we can avoid that?"

She looked at him with a smirk, then at the room. "It's about the user. We shape it to protect, not rule. That's what I've worked for, and that's what I'm here to teach."

Paul stood, grabbing his notebook to leave. "Then we can't mess it up."

October 31$^{st}$ 6:45 p.m. -Arizona Dessert

The Council chamber rose victoriously from the Arizona desert, stark against dusk, walls carved with Trinity symbolism. Sarah sat at the table's head, her authority clear, though she answered to Zar'vok, her alien elder. He sat beside her, listening as she led. Diplomats and emissaries reviewed papers as Sarah spoke. "These rules are permanent. They say we're one team, many species."

Zar'vok speaks. "The Trinity holds us. Human will, alien wisdom, shared bond. That's our strength."

Sarah pointed to the documents. "We're making it official. The Convergence failed by forcing things. We succeed by working together."

Zar'vok stood, his golden rod tapped the floor, gathering attention. "For eons, the Trinity has guarded free will across the galaxies, a divine gift we've sworn to protect. These attacks on earth, this attack born of 9/11, are but stories of an older war... those who worship control seek to break that sacred balance. Let it stand. Worlds unite through trust, not force. Tech serves. Peace lasts."

Sarah watched him with admiration. She'd joined young, a hybrid unsure, guided by Zar'vok through years of mentorship. Now they stood together, their vision as one. The Council agreed. This was built to last.

October 31$^{st}$ 7:11 p.m. -Washington D.C.

Paul sat holding a worn leather wallet. Inside was his father's old military insignia, a tie to a man who left early. He kept it, a quiet piece of his past. Amy joined him. They sat in silence, comfortable.

He pocketed the wallet. "I'll explain this sometime," he said, smiling. "Things are feeling right again."

"They are." Amy said. "The world, the Council, us—it's clicking. The Mindlink could too, if I get it right."

"I know you will," Paul said.

They stayed there, ready to meet the future side by side.

# Twenty-Three
## *The Battle Within*

The Pentagon War Room was full of good early morning attitudes. Paul stood at the table's head, commanding the room. Data showed connections between government insiders, rogue aliens, and terrorists. Secret dealings they'd fought to expose. Amy and Farid were there, standing as backup, friends in this together, supporting him as part of the team.

Paul made a noise with his throat. "Today we end this. The government used alien technology we built with Amy's lab for nefarious means. They wanted to harm people, to control them, turning folks into cogs and slaves for the elites. They tried to take away free will, the one thing God gave us to choose for ourselves." He rested his fist lightly on the table, a show of commitment. "We stand against that because free will matters. Our resolve must keep going."

Amy said what everyone was thinking, "We need to tread lightly, Paul. The truth could ignite unrest."

He argued, "They deserve to know. The lies we found out, our alliances, it all comes out now."

November 1st 9:30 a.m. -Washington D.C.

After the busy briefing that morning, Paul, Amy, and Farid sought out a quiet space in the Pentagon to watch a broadcast. They settled into an office and turned on the screen. Recorded videos showed peaceful alien colonies working alongside humans, families sharing values and peace.

Farid said, "They deserve this story. I know what it's like to be caught in the middle."

Paul said, "The world sees it now. They'll have to choose what comes next."

The lie ended.

November 1st 11:00 a.m. -Washington D.C.

A staffer led them to a secure room where the team dismantled the dissidents' network, jotting notes and marking red flags. A transmission crackled through. "This is field ops," a voice said. "Paperwork's coming, but here's the heads-up: we've got footage from airports and backroads. Rogue aliens directed terrorists from those grounded 9/11 planes—ones that never hit their targets—to hide. Caught them on camera meeting up, slipping away."

A second update followed. "Osama Bin Laden's still free. Spotted in Pakistan, pacing a tiny compound, waiting for orders and biding his time."

A third. Twenty-three people so far, found with installed Mindlinks.

Paul shook his head in disbelief. "Is this ever going to end? They almost won. Bin Laden's still out there, and at least one other terrorist."

Paul was not in the mood and the reports blurred together. September 11$^{th}$ wasn't the goal, it was the crack in the dam. The real plan was control, a world where the Mindlink chained every thought, where the divine spark—the Trinity, whatever that meant, went dark. And they were closer than he'd feared."

Amy said, "He's hiding now, Paul. It's a long fight ahead, but I'm on it until I find him."

"We'll get him," Paul said. "They tried to pervert creation itself, but good already won."

Farid said, "The Mindlink technology helped us trace that signal. Amy's work is making a difference."

Amy replied, "I'll make sure it's never used to harm again. That's my line in the sand."


November 2nd 1:30 p.m. -Arizona Dessert

Paul, Amy, and Farid arrived in Arizona for the Council meeting. Peaceful aliens filled the chamber, planning the earth's future. Their tech had stopped the Convergence, and now they figured out what came next.

Sarah said, "We've come far, but now we face a choice: do we stay separate or integrate with humanity?"

There was some discussion.

Paul said, "The old one, the Convergence of evil, is gone. We shape what's next. This tech, human and alien, can create perfect peace if we use it right."

Sarah said, "Our beliefs vary, but peace binds us."

Zar'vok stood, leaning on his rod. Paul studied it, realizing it was one of the Trinity's relics—the missing piece he'd wondered about. "We'll create a new convergence," Zar'vok said, "one for good, built on peace and unity across all worlds."

Amy said, "I'm so glad to help with Mindlink to bridge our communications."

Paul took his eyes off the golden rod and looked at Zar'vok. "This alliance promises more than survival. It's our foundation."

November 4th 3:19 p.m. -Washington D.C.

The day was dragging on. Paul and Amy walked the Pentagon grounds. Paul paused. "Amy, you've been amazing through all this. I'm lucky to have you on this team."

Amy smiled. "We're in it together."

Paul sensed she was nudging him and asked, "Together as in you and me? As in us?"

Amy smiled again. "Yes."

November 4<sup>th</sup> 4:30 p.m. -Washington D.C.

In the final debrief of the day, the team explained the technology used to stop the convergence. Alien technology played a crucial role, combined with AI systems human scientists developed in secret.

General Davis addresses the group and announced the defeat of evil. "What steps can we take to ensure this never happens again?" he asked.

Paul hollered out, ready to be done with the day. "We continue working with the Council, build a long-term partnership with the peaceful alien factions, global leaders, and keep improving our defenses. Earth and the galaxy may stay separate for now, but we're on the path to converge.

November 4<sup>th</sup> 9:30 p.m. -Northern Virginia

Paul, Amy, and Farid need to let off some steam. They'd been through hell, and a pub in Georgetown seemed like the perfect place to decompress, maybe laugh a little, shake it off. The place was happening with music and good drinks. They grabbed a table, finally able to relax.

Amy raised her glass. "Here's to normal."

Paul touched his glass to hers. "We stopped them."

Farid, a little buzzed, grinned wide. "I'm not just surviving. I'm living!"

They salute, soaking in the moment.

# Twenty-Four
## *Last Stand*

The tribunal room, a reminder of the wreckage that brought them here. Soldiers, intelligence officials, and world leaders filled the seats, their eyes on Brian Strohm. He sat in the center, head high, defiance radiating despite the verdict hanging over him. Paul Keogh watched from the back, arms crossed, as the military tribunal prepared to judge the man who nearly shattered the world. Brian stole advanced technology meant for humanity, used corrupt governments, and betrayed everyone for power. Now, justice closed in.

The prosecutor's tone was cold and matter-of-fact. "Brian Strohm, you stole and hoarded alien technology for your own gain. You endangered millions, human and alien alike."

"But your ambitions went far beyond personal gain. Evidence uncovered in your private servers reveals a chilling truth. You sought to weaponize Convergence, using the Mindlink technology, you were trusted to head up. You attempted to dominate humanity. Your plan wasn't just power, was it? 9/11 was the opening move—a way to fracture humanity's spirit. Your plan was to erode free will itself, enslaving entire populations to serve your vision of a new order."

Paul peaked at Amy beside him, her focus on the proceedings. They had survived months of unimaginable trials. Farid stayed on Paul's mind, recovering from the implant's torment. Paul didn't want to admit it to Farid, but he saw the change in him. Even with the implant removal, it had already left its mark.

Anticipation gripped the room as the prosecutor detailed Brian's crimes—secret pacts with corrupt aliens, control over elites, a war waged in hidden battles. Everyone awaited the hammer of judgment. The prosecutor turned. "Mr. Keogh, your statement?"

Paul walked up, tension grew as stiff as a diving board. "You thought you could control it all." Paul said. "You used me, Amy and Farid. You played with lives. For what?"

Brian smirked. "You don't know what's coming, Paul. The convergence you think you stopped. This is just the start."

Brian's words really got to Paul, but he handled it better than most would have. "You tried to forge a convergence of evil, corrupt aliens and humans bent to your will. You failed. Now, we will build a convergence for peace. Without you."

Brian's smile was gone, yet his arrogance hung on. "You're blind, Keogh. Forces beyond you are moving."

Paul approached, coming face to face. "We are done here." Pleased, he sat back down without looking back.

Guards escorted Brian out, his head high. Paul knew Brian's time was done, even if his ego refused to yield.

His defiance never wavered; his head held high as though he believed history would vindicate him. But Paul knew better. The world had changed, and Brian's time was over.

The tribunal head called for order.

Paul and Amy watched soldiers load Brian into a transport bound for a maximum-security prison. His life sentence was sealed. "He still thinks he won something," Paul said as the vehicle rolled away.

Amy nodded. "At least he's gone now." November's fresh air brushed their faces as they began to walk and talk.

The world beyond remained oblivious to the deeper truth, all of it buried beneath 9/11's aftermath. Paul's mind went to the new Global Peace Council. Brian's fall left a void, and nations scrambled for the alien secrets he exposed. The struggle for power went on.

November 21$^{st}$ 1:15 p.m. -Arizona Dessert

As a symbol of unity, the newly renamed Global Peace Council's Arizona headquarters thrives with joy and productivity. Scientists worked on equations, diplomats studied plans, and aliens tinkered with holographic displays. Side by side, humans and aliens constructed a common future.

Paul and Amy arrived, greeted by Sarah, the new Council leader, bridging both species. "We're building something here," Sarah said, leading them into the main hall. "Earth and the stars, working as one. This is more than survival, it's progress. And that makes me happy."

United humans and aliens filled Paul's view. This fragile yet real future—this is what they fought for.

Sarah spoke again. "Not everyone agrees. We must give it time. Some leaders view this as a threat. They won't surrender control easily."

Amy adds. "Power clings hard."

Paul asked, "Will it hold?"

"For now," Sarah said. "We stay vigilant."

November 21st 7:33 p.m. -Washington D.C.

Back in Washington, Paul and Amy walked the Pentagon grounds, the city still healing from the attack. Reconstruction was going full force. "We honor the lost by rebuilding," Amy said. "New York, the Pentagon, we make sure it never happens again." Paul felt that. That tragic day sparked it all—alien discoveries, conspiracies, battles. Now, peace felt within reach, earned through sacrifice. Normal was worth it.

November 22nd 11:58 a.m. -Washington D.C.

Caught up in the briefing room, Paul, Amy, and Farid studied reports. They decided to spend Thanksgiving week getting organized. Aliens they had yet to capture were regrouping. Osama Bin Laden hid, clutching technology not meant for him. "We stopped the worst," Paul said. "But they're waiting to strike again."

Farid happy, bandages marking his temple from the implant's removal. "I'm free of it," he said, giving a smile.

Amy took notice. "You sure you're OK?" Farid assured them, but Paul and Amy saw that he was different, quieter, the implant's curse clinging despite its absence.

Paul took command of the conversation, changing the unspoken topic. "They're out there, but we're ready. The Trinity will guide us forward."

December 23$^{rd}$ 5:07 a.m. -Northern Virginia

On either side of the bed, Paul and Amy's phones rang, causing them to jump awake. They grabbed them in the dark. A message from the new Secretary of Defense flashed: "Urgent. Holograms appearing globally. Unknown origin. Report to work."

Paul sat up, alert. Amy was already dressing. "You ready?" she asked.

"Yeah," he said. "Let's go."

They dressed fast, packed some food and overnight supplies, knowing their place in the world. As they stepped out, Paul said, "The Convergence of Evil is done. This is something else."

December 23rd 5:58 a.m. -Washington D.C.

Washington, decked out for Christmas, was the backdrop to Paul and Amy's predawn drive to the Pentagon. Visions of sacred places had popped up worldwide—Death Valley, Europe, underwater Australia,

Flor China, Russia, sudden and unexplained. No one knew their source or who controlled them.

The Trinity... human, alien, and the divine had lit their path. It would shine on. The world kept turning.

The future stretched out, uncertain but theirs to shape.

# In remembrance

This section contains historical images from the tragic events of September 11, 2001 — a day that changed the course of history and left an indelible mark on the hearts of Americans and people around the world.

The photographs presented here were sourced with permission from the U.S. National Archives and Records Administration, and are used with the utmost respect and acknowledgment of the lives lost, the survivors, the heroes, and the families forever impacted.

Though this book is a work of fiction, the events of 9/11 are real — and this project does not seek to diminish their gravity or sacredness. These images are included to ground the story in the reality from which it draws inspiration, and to honor those whose lives were forever altered by this act of terror.

We remember.

We honor.

We will never forget.

Twin Towers in NYC Septemeber 11<sup>th</sup> Attack

President George W. Bush with Bob Beckwith,
rallying NYC Fire and Rescue

President George W. Bush on the phone aboard Air
Force One on Sept. 11, 2001

Resilience at the Pentagon

September 11, 2001, American Airlines Flight 77, hijacked by terrorists, crashed into the west side of the Pentagon, killing 184 people inside and on the plane.

Flight 93 crashed into an open field in Somerset County, Pennsylvania, killing all passengers, crew members, and terrorists on board.

World Trade Center after the attack. Makeshift
Memorials were everywhere.

Emergency & News crews in NYC